"The man
who fights
for his
ideals
is the man
who
is alive."
CERVANTES
author of
DON QUIXOTE
Jack Hodson
January 13, 1978

ALSO BY VLADIMIR VOINOVICH

•

THE LIFE AND

EXTRAORDINARY ADVENTURES OF

PRIVATE IVAN CHONKIN

(1977)

THE IVANKIAD

Janusz Zalewski

VLADIMIR
VOINOVICH

THE IVANKIAD

OR
THE TALE
OF THE WRITER
VOINOVICH'S
INSTALLATION
IN HIS NEW
APARTMENT

TRANSLATED BY DAVID LAPEZA

FARRAR, STRAUS AND GIROUX
NEW YORK

Russian text first published by Ardis under the title, Иванькиада,

Printed in the United States of America
Designed by Cynthia Krupat
First printing, 1977
Portions of the text originally appeared in
The New York Times Magazine
Library of Congress Cataloging in Publication Data
Voĭnovich, Vladimir / The Ivankiad
Translation of Ivan'kiada, ili rasskaz o vselenii
pisatelia Voĭnovicha v novuiu kvartiru.
1. Voinovich, Vladimir, 1932– / –Biography.
2. Authors, Russian–20th century–Biography. I. Title.
PG3489.4.I53Z5213 / 891.7'3'44 [B] / 77-5642

Dedicated to

Sergei Sergeevich Ivanko

and his comrades,

who placed at the author's disposal,

free of charge,

the richest factual material

and food for thought

In Place of a Foreword

Before this whole thing happened, I was peacefully writing my *Chonkin*, intending to finish it "this year." I had just managed to get out of one mess, and by certain indications I could tell I'd soon be in another. There would be renewed nervous strain, and absolutely no money, and I figured that right now, while there was a little left over after paying my debts (by some miracle two books had come out at the same time), I would have to write *Chonkin* as quickly as possible and not get distracted by anything extraneous. But the extraneous crept in without being asked and distracted me anyway. Unexpectedly I became involved in a long and absurd struggle over the expansion of my living space. Frankly, this isn't characteristic of me. As much as possible I try to avoid any struggle for my personal well-being. I hate going to the authorities and making an effort to get things. I am by nature undemanding, content with very little. I am no gourmet, no dandy, and have no interest in luxury items. Simple food, modest clothes, and a roof over my head, that's all I need for a sense of well-being. True, under that roof I've always wanted to have a separate room all for myself, but such a desire could scarcely be considered excessive.

So, in spite of my character, I suddenly became part of a desperate struggle. For several months *Chonkin* was completely forgotten. For several months I spent all my time writing letters and applications, making the rounds of authorities, making phone calls, gathering supporters, dissembling, getting angry, losing my temper, consuming several packets of Seduxin and Tyleval. It was only thanks to my basically good health that I got through this stuggle without a heart attack. I tried to maintain my composure, but I wasn't always able to. What saved me was that at a certain point I decided that one must look at everything with a sense of humor, since all knowledge is a blessing. I calmed down; my hatred gave way to curiosity, which was satisfied by my adversary, who revealed himself as if in a striptease. I was no longer struggling. I was gathering material for this work, and my adversary and his pals actively helped me, outlining this terrific plot, making a series of moves which you would not be able to think up over the dinner table. This plot is not merely fascinating; it explains, I think, certain phenomena in our country which are not always understood, either here or abroad.

To give an example: perhaps you can understand why they don't publish *The Gulag Archipelago:* for this it would be necessary to change internal politics completely. But, for the publication of a book like *Doctor Zhivago*, nothing has to be changed. They could just publish it openly in an edition equal to the demand, collect an adequate profit, and dispense forever with the question "Why isn't that novel published in your country?" Why not allow an artist, even the most abstract, to display his pictures in some vacant lot? Could he really budge the power of our government even a millimeter? You don't think so? I don't either. So why smash the picture with a bulldozer? That's uncultured, and expensive, too. Add up the depreciation on the bulldozer, double-time (for a holiday) for the driver, and the price of everyone's soup goes up.*

I purposely do not touch on the moral side of these

* Things have changed for the better now. The authorities have permitted several exhibitions of the so-called unofficial artists, and although a few works (for example, the artist Odnoralov's overcoat) struck uninitiated viewers as perhaps a little unusual, our government withstood this shock, and stands as firmly on its feet as it did before. (V.V.)

questions. I speak only of expediency. I ask: Why does our super-government so often act against itself without any apparent reason?

Western Sovietologists and even a few of our own thinkers explain everything by dogmatic Marxism. As if some faithful and orthodox dogmatist sits in his office armchair and, holding Marx by the beard with one hand, leafs through *Das Kapital* with the other, checking his every step against it. Right?

I can't say anything definite about Marx, I've never read him. But in this, my fifth decade of living in this country and looking closely at our life, I seem to have lost sight of this orthodox person. Apparently he died quietly and was buried without honors. But from a rosy mirage there arises before me not a dogmatist, not an orthodox person, but a figure of a new type. I hasten to present him to you, dear reader.

V. V.

PART I

To study life you don't have to go on creative junkets and waste public funds. Study life where you live, it's more productive, and cheaper, too. For example, just look around our courtyard. Look at the kind of people there are—what types, what fates! Probably you can also find interesting people at KAMAZ or BAM,* but not to such a degree as here.

Our building isn't really anything special, but you can't say it's ordinary either. The engineers of the human soul† live here, the members of the Moscow Writers' Housing Cooperative. There are quite a number of people in this world who have never seen a single living writer in their entire lives. But we've got more than a hundred of them. The well-known, the little-known, the totally unknown, Rich, poor, talented, original, undistinguished, left, right, middle, and uncommitted. They've known each other for decades. In days gone by they used to eat each other; now they live peacefully under one roof, both those who did the eating, and those who were eaten—but only partially.

See that old man hurrying across the courtyard with his bobbing gait, pathetic, feeble, thin as a dandelion? True, the fluff has already blown off this dandelion—the little head nods on a thin neck stem. You're sorry for the old man? They say he was once the Procurator General of the Ukraine and had four stars on his collar. Not everyone who met up with the dandelion in that glorious time lived long enough to be able to feel sorry for him. And the one who is now supporting the dandelion by the elbow?

* Acronyms for the latest Soviet large-scale construction projects.

† Ironic allusion to Stalin's "Writers are the engineers of the human soul."

He used to wear ties, not neckties, mind you, but the kind that go around one's shoulders, which were used to lead him anywhere the dandelion (not yet blown bare) wanted him to go.

What can you say; all kinds of people live in our building, people with the oddest biographies. Descendants of aristocratic families, former Bolsheviks, Mensheviks, Chekists, Trotskyites, deviationists, Stalin Prize winners, cosmopolites, orthodox people, revisionists, secretaries of the Writers' Union—and that's not all.

Not so long ago, Galich* walked from doorway to doorway, and Bek† asked of everyone he met, "Well, what do they say of my novel?"

Some are no longer here, others are further away.

Arkady Vasiliev, Chekist, writer, prosecutor of Sinyavsky and Daniel, also lived in our building. Now he doesn't live here. Now he lies in Novodevichny Cemetery between Kochetov and Tvardovsky, not far from Khrushchev.

Everything is mixed up.

But still, not everyone died and not everyone went away. There are interesting people in our building even now. Hang around our courtyard and you might meet Simonov‡ himself.

And here's another character: an auntie, not in her first youth, who runs around the courtyard smoking long cigarettes and defiantly using uncensored words, and who carries in her shopping bag . . . you'd never guess . . . it's terrible to say . . . it takes my breath away . . . *The Gulag Archipelago*. Loudly and openly offering to let

* Alexander Galich: writer, dramatist, song composer. Exiled from the Soviet Union in 1974.

† Alexander Bek: author of dreary documentary novels.

‡ Konstantin Simonov: prominent and prolific writer, winner of the Stalin Prize.

everyone read it. Heavens, what's going on in our courtyard if people openly carry around subversive literature? And where is our whistle? Isn't it about time someone blew the whistle? No hurry, this woman will take you to the place you should visit on occasion anyway—that's where she got the book. And she offers it to you, not for nothing, but so that, after you get acquainted with the special paragraphs on General Vlasov,* you'll write a statement for the newspaper—an unfavorable one, of course.

Suppose you refuse: "Well, you know, I'd be only too happy to, but as it happens I'm on my way to Novosibirsk right now . . ." and you start digging in your pockets, searching for those tickets you didn't buy. That's all right, our auntie isn't offended; she runs after some other comrade, perhaps his train hasn't arrived yet. There, a man's running after her, let him read it, or just sign the statement without reading it . . . he hasn't published for a long time, he just has to squeeze his name in somewhere, but no, he's not grown up yet; authoritative writers, writers with names, are needed for this job.

But if you just want to do some public speaking and proclaim "Here I am," you need only wait for the next assembly of the shareholders in the cooperative. There we have almost complete democracy. You want to express yourself, just raise your hand, they'll notice you and give you the floor, not like in the Writers' Union.

These assemblies, as a rule, are stormy. Insatiable social passions boil, spears clash, warring groups rise and disband.

•

* General Vlasov: commander of the Second Army, who was taken prisoner in July 1942 and fought on the side of the Nazis against the Soviet Army.

At one of these assemblies, on January 27, 1973, to be precise, I first heard the name of the man who was destined to become the hero of these notes. I remember that assembly, primarily because it was decided there who was to get the two-room apartment that was vacant. There were two claimants—the author of these lines, and a certain Pavel Lipatov, the writer Vorobiev's wife's son. Supporters spoke from both sides. One of those who spoke in my favor called upon the assembly to consider the mistakes of the past, and to take care of writers while they are still alive. Since the speaker was an emotional man, he surprised everyone, and perhaps even himself, when he compared what was happening with an event of much greater import.

"I remember," he said, "the torture of Pasternak . . ." Most likely Pasternak's torture didn't do any good. The assembly was basically on my side, and later, when it came to a vote, granted me the apartment by an overwhelming majority. I refused the apartment in favor of Lipatov, since he was first in line, but asked the assembly to confirm my right to the next two-room apartment. The assembly supported my request unanimously, as was recorded in the minutes.

I would not have mentioned this unimportant event if it did not have some significance for the further development of our plot.

But now let us return to my supporter's speech. So, he said, "I remember the torture of Pasternak . . ."

He was not allowed to complete his sentence. From the back row rose a well-fed, middle-aged man in a white knit shirt, with an uninteresting face that would be hard to remember. His sparse hair, though combed from one side to the other and carefully arranged, still did not entirely cover the crown of his head.

"As a Communist," he said, not looking at anyone, "I protest the words 'the torture of Pasternak.' "

Having said this, the man sat down in his place and turned indifferently toward the window. It seemed as if his statement was made without any enthusiasm, not in a burst of indignation, but so that no one could reproach him for having been there, heard such words, and remained silent.

Those present at the assembly turned their heads toward the man in surprise; there was a slight hesitation, and then everything proceeded normally.

After the meeting I asked someone who that vigilant Communist was. They told me, some Ivánko or Ivankó, a member of the board of our cooperative. I was completely satisfied with the answer and immediately forgot about the man.

I did not know that, before a month passed, fate would bring me together with this man, and that for a long time he would occupy all my thoughts and fire my curiosity.

Aaron Kuperstock Departs for His Historic Homeland

Hurrah! Hurrah! The writer Andrei Klenov (actually Aaron Kuperstock) has received permission to leave for Israel. He will be vacating a two-room apartment. They say it's an excellent apartment. Rooms of seventeen square meters with windows on both sides, and two balconies . . . The patience of my wife and myself has been rewarded. For five years we have lived in a one-room apartment, for five years we have waited our turn. Our one-room apartment is the only one in the whole building. We have waited longer than the others, we have greater need than the others, we will get this apartment. Our right to it is indisputable and was confirmed by the last assembly. Now I will have my own room, where in blessed silence I will be able to create my works, immortal or otherwise. Just imagine, a separate room! As long as I've lived, I've never known such luxury. If some kind magician were to appear and ask my one desire, I would say, "I want a room to myself."

•

Walking around the courtyard, I met a certain wise man (whose name I shall omit). He said, "Be careful you don't let Klenov's apartment slip."

"Why should I be careful if there aren't any real claimants to that apartment besides me?"

"You think so?" He laughed. "I know Klenov's apartment. It's a very good apartment. Do you want my opinion?"

"Well?"

"You will get the apartment, but with very great difficulty."

"You know something?"

"I know one fact: it's a very good apartment, and it's not possible that there isn't someone who covets it."

I walked on. Shaking his head, the translator Yakov Kozlovsky ran to meet me. He always has the air of a dog sniffing something out, afraid that some passerby might hit him with a stick. He spoke in his usual manner—cowering, looking over his shoulder, whispering: "Listen, old man, don't get your hopes up, you won't get that apartment."

"Why not?"

He looked around again (someone following?). "Old man, I've told you everything I can."

And, leaving me perplexed, he ran off.

Against my will, I began to get worried. Something was going on with that vacant apartment, intrigues were being spun. At every step I was meeting well-wishers who forewarned me. "You have to keep your eyes open, you should put up a fight."

Why fight, and who with? Where was the opponent I would have to knock out?

From My Diary

February 13. The board meeting of the cooperative is set for tomorrow. I went to one of the board members to ask if he would stand up for me.

"You know," I said, "it's sort of awkward for me to notify everyone, but if you on the board are deciding this matter and some complications should come up, please keep in mind that, besides everything else, my wife is pregnant, only in her third month, but I have enough other rights to it anyway. Let this be just one more argument in my favor."

•

February 14. In the evening there was a ring at the door. The board member I had visited came in.

"Here's what, my children," he said to my wife and me. "We just met. I'm afraid I must disappoint you. It looks like you won't get Klenov's apartment. But never mind, they'll give you Bazhova's apartment. True, it's not as good—the rooms are small and all on one side—but it's still a two-roomer."

I didn't understand at all. Who was this Bazhova? Why should I get an apartment she was still living in and not Klenov's, which was vacant?

Our guest explained. Boris Alexandrovich Turganov, the Chairman of the cooperative, had spoken. He had said there was a mistake in the building's design. There was only one one-room apartment in the building. However, there were children growing up, some of them wanting to split off, to move out. For example, Bazhova wants to separate from her son and change her two-room apartment into two one-roomers. So, if we separate one room from Kuperstock's apartment—Turganov pronounces Klenov's real name painstakingly and with obvious implication—one room with a kitchen, bath, and toilet will be left, i.e., a one-room apartment. After that, everything is simple: Voinovich moves into Bazhova's apartment, Bazhova gets Voinovich's apartment and the one left over from Kuperstock's apartment.

I still didn't understand. What was the problem? Why should it be necessary to make a one-room apartment out of a two-room apartment? And what would happen to the room left over, without kitchen, bath, or toilet?

It turned out that the whole crux of the matter was this leftover room. Sergei Sergeevich Ivanko had requested an improvement in his living conditions: the addition of this room to his apartment.

I still didn't get it. How was this Ivanko so badly off? Did he have a poor apartment? No, he had a three-room apartment for three people, one of the best in our building. Perhaps he had waited a long time? No, he had lived in our building a shorter time than others, since 1969, and in October of last year he put in an application for an improvement in his living conditions, requesting a fourth room. Why did he request a fourth room? On what basis? You can request anything you like. I, too, could request four rooms, but no one would give them to me.

"You told them my wife is expecting?"

"Yes, of course," said my interlocutor. "What's more, I said: 'I understand, perhaps our respected colleague Sergei Sergeevich really does need this room, but then Voinovich lives in a one-room apartment and his wife is pregnant. Sergei Sergeevich, wouldn't you feel uncomfortable in a luxurious four-room apartment knowing that your comrade, a writer, is huddled with his wife and child in one room?' "

"And what did he say?" I burst out.

"Him? He smiled sweetly and said, 'Well, I'd manage to get over it.' "

At that I just threw up my hands. "He said it just like that?"

"Yes," our guest replied, embarrassed, "said it just like that."

"You, of course, were indignant? You told him he was going too far?"

"No." Our guest was even more embarrassed. "I didn't say anything. I was stunned."

You were stunned!

Another question came to mind. "And what about this Bazhova, does she understand that in our building two one-room apartments will cost twice as much as one two-roomer? I suppose she's a millionaire?"

"No, she's rather poor, but Ivanko says he'll help her."

"You mean, just buy one of the apartments for her?"

"Most likely."

"And he's paying for the room he wants, too?"

"And for breaking through the main wall."

"Then he's a millionaire?"

"At any rate, he doesn't spare expense."

"But breaking a main wall is strictly forbidden, by architectural regulations."

"He says they'll let him."

"Just who is he?"

"I don't know who he is. A writer, most likely. They say he's a member of the Writers' Union."

"And what am I, in your opinion?"

"Volodya, why badger me?" said our guest, getting angry. "I'm telling you what happened. Since he talks that way, it means he figures he can get away with it."

"But what do the other members of the board say? Besides you, there are some decent people there. So you were stunned, what about them?"

"They were stunned, too."

•

Our guest departed, and my wife and I were left in complete confusion. What a disaster! Where had this writer come from? The writer Ivanko. I still have some contact with that profession, follow the new literary figures, but God strike me if I've ever heard that name before. I grabbed the directory of the Writers' Union, opened to the necessary letter: Ivanovich, Ivanter, Ivasyuk, not even a mention of Ivanko here. If he wasn't in the directory, that meant he was only recently admitted. So he must be a young writer. Why such indulgences for a young writer? He should live in four rooms while I stay in one? Of course, we should be concerned about the up-and-coming literary generation, but not to such an extent!

And how was I to take his statement that he would get over it?

Once, in the first hungry postwar year, the author of these lines studied in a trade school to become a professional carpenter. We got three free meals a day. Usually we all ate breakfast and midday dinner, but not everyone got supper. We swooped down like kites upon the waitress with her tray and grabbed for the food. Some got two portions, some got three, and some none at all. This system of distribution of the social product bore the name "on the grab." But it was hungry children who were acting that way, and only when the foreman or some other superior wasn't around.

But this was in broad daylight, in front of the very

eyes of the writers' community. What was going on? Ring all the bells immediately! Where was our Chairman's telephone number?

A Figure of Regional Fame

I did not set the portrayal of Boris Alexandrovich Turganov as my goal, but, unfortunately, we cannot get by without him in this story. Therefore, allow me, at least in passing, to present him to you. He is, as I already informed you, the Chairman of our housing cooperative. A translator from the Ukrainian. Age: around seventy. Head as bare as an egg. Walks about the courtyard importantly, speaks impressively, shows by his entire appearance what a big man he is, what serious problems he has to solve in everyday life. They say that once in private conversation he said, "No matter what you say, the Chairman of the writers' cooperative cuts a figure on the regional level."

Boris Alexandrovich pronounces the names of officials and the titles of their offices with youthful delight. He prefers to speak of himself in the third person:

"So what do you want—the Chairman to think for you?"

"I beg you to watch your language. You are in the Chairman's presence."

I write Boris Alexandrovich's title of office with a capital letter, following the style he uses. He designates all offices, beginning with his own and higher, only with capital letters.

An acquaintance of mine is renowned for his remarkable memory and for the fact that he knows almost everyone in Moscow who has anything to do with literature, and he loves to give a short characterization of each one as he comes up in conversation. His descriptions are benevolent as a rule. For example, you ask him what Ivanov is like.

"Ivanov?" he asks back. "A very talented man."

Or, a very good man, an attractive man, a successful man, a pretty good man, a not untalented man, etc.

To my question about Turganov, he said without hesitation, "A very rich man." And after a moment's thought, he added, "And a very bad man."

We shall, perhaps, return to a portrait of our Chairman, but for now, I will tell you only that then, on the evening of February 14, I called him on the telephone. His wife answered. After finding out who was asking for her husband, she said, "I'll just go look, I think he's already gone to bed." And, after a pause, "Yes, he's gone to bed."

I called in the morning.

"Boris Alexandrovich is still sleeping."

I called again, a little while later.

"He's just gone out."

"I thought so," I said. "Never mind, I'll find him anyway."

In the late afternoon, the telephone rang.

"Vladimir Nikolaevich, this is Turganov. I'm calling so you won't think I'm hiding from you. Why do you think the board shouldn't consider some alternatives?"

"If it has the time, the board can consider anything it likes. But apartment 66 should belong to me. Especially since, as you remember, it was decided at the last assembly."

"There was no such decision. It was a recommendation."

"Boris Alexandrovich, you know very well that only the board can make recommendations. The assembly does not make recommendations, it makes decisions. I understand what dictates your actions, but it's not worth it for you to fight for this, you won't get it. You won't push it through the assembly, and without the assembly, you won't get very far, I promise you. If you are a sensible man, you should understand that." Silence. "Do you agree with me?"

He did not answer my question. After a pause he said, "I know who told you about the board meeting."

From these words I concluded that Turganov looks upon our cooperative's board as a secret society which must keep its affairs a mystery to the rank-and-file shareholders.

He's No Bureaucratic Hack

I was spared the necessity of gathering information on Ivanko—reports on him rained down on me. Various people made these reports, some with threats, others just casually. In the end, I learned that Ivanko, Sergei Sergeevich, born 1925, was:

a. A relative of the former director of the KGB, Semichastny.

b. A close friend of Nikolai T. Fedorenko, the former Soviet representative to the United Nations, now editor in chief of the journal *Inostrannaya Literatura* (*Foreign Literature*) and secretary of the Writers' Union of the U.S.S.R.

c. A big shot in his own right. He managed some sort of publishing department in the United Nations, and is now a member of the board of Goskomizdat, which is in charge of all the publishing houses in the Soviet Union; thus, he can shoot down any book he wants in any one of them. Besides that—so they say—he has a considerable position in that same institution of which his relative Semichastny was director, and not only can shoot down a book but without great difficulty can be the death of the author as well.

Sober men advised me to yield.

A few things had become clear, but others were not so intelligible. If he was such a big man, why didn't they give him a state apartment the size he needed?

"They'd give him anything he wants, but he can't move out of here."

"Why not?"

"Because, as he says himself, he equipped this apartment. He brought a stove from America, a toilet, an air conditioner, special wallpaper, some other special stuff, and all this has been stuck into the walls, the floors, the ceilings. Equipping an apartment costs an enormous amount of money, and to tear it all out would wreck it. He can't move anywhere, he can only spread out or break through above or below."

"Vladimir Nikolaevich," the elevator lady* from Ivanko's entranceway said to me, "did you see when he moved in?" (She avoided mentioning my rival by name.) "No? Well, we did. Two trucks with containers, and everything American. The toilet, the stove, the devil knows what. A sled, even a child's sled, he brought that from America, too!" For some reason that sled made the greatest impression on her. "Why, Vladimir Nikolaevich, five rooms would be too small for him."

"Yes," said the writer M., "I also saw the way he moved in. It was an impressive sight for these parts: a mass of objects of unknown use, each covered with foil and on each in large letters IVANKO." (He pronounced it in the English manner, with a hard *n*.)

"But they say he put in an application for improvements in October, before anyone knew that Klenov would leave. What was he counting on then?"

"At that time he was counting on one of Kozlovsky's rooms."

* In most Soviet apartment houses there is a woman who sits by the elevator—not to run it, but to check who enters and leaves.

"What?" I hadn't lost the ability to be surprised. "But Kozlovsky is still living in his apartment."

"Don't you understand, you crazy man? That doesn't mean anything to Ivanko."

Indeed! Nothing matters to him!

"Listen," someone asked Kozlovsky, "what did Ivanko have in mind when he put in an application for your room?"

"Don't ask, don't talk about it," said Kozlovsky, frightened and cowering. "He probably wants to send me off to Israel or have me shot or something."

These are the first strokes in our portrait of Sergei Sergeevich Ivanko.

•

But here is the same picture in a different light. The speaker is a middle-aged lady, the wife of one of the most influential members of the board of our cooperative.

"My dear, you speak of Sergei Sergeevich unjustly. He's a very good, a very kind man. I understand your position, but you must understand his. He brought all that equipment from America, and even if right now they offered him five rooms in the New Arbat, the fanciest section of Moscow, he couldn't take them. Yes, he's a very attractive man. Some say that he's a bureaucratic hack, but he isn't one at all. He's a writer. Yes, he's a writer. And he doesn't even have his own study."

My God, you just feel like crying over the unhappy fate of this writer Ivanko. It's become almost awkward somehow. As if I have a study, a living room, a bedroom, a dining room, and as if I'm trying to take something away from him, not he from me.

"But he has three rooms for three people," I said, a bit timidly. "Why can't he make one room a study?"

"My dear, can't you understand?" She was simply staggered by my stupidity and heartlessness. "I tell you, his apartment is all equipped. He literally doesn't have enough room to turn around in. You are a human being. Why can't you put yourself in another human being's place? Yes, I understand, you live in one room and don't have a study either, and your wife . . . By the way, you tell her that she shouldn't worry at this time. And don't you be nervous. We'll find something for you, without fail. My husband says that you want only a really good apartment, that you won't even hear of Bazhova's apartment. What's wrong with you? Vera Ivanovna Bunina . . . Do you know her? No? As it happens, she thinks very highly of you. She promised to find you a good apartment. Just be patient for two days, Vera Ivanovna will find you something. Klenov's apartment belongs to you, it's yours, but just for two days. Sergei Sergeevich is such a kind man. I don't know him very well, but he is very attractive. Certainly not a bureaucratic hack. Go home, my dear, calm down, and calm your wife. She shouldn't be worrying now."

This monologue was delivered (and noted down at home) on February 15.

And here's yet another view:

"Ivanko a writer? What are you talking about? This saucepan's more of a writer. A regular Akaky Akakievich.* I know him inside out, worked with him on *Literature and Life*. They sacked him later on. During the time of our great friendship with China, he wrote a lead article about it and made a political gaffe. He said there had been an "upsurge in the economies of the U.S.A. and China."

One more opinion:

"What do you mean? He's no Akaky Akakievich, he's an important figure. Once he really was very kind and

* The office-dwelling, pen-pushing hero of Gogol's "The Overcoat."

affable. But then he went to America and came back all puffed up."

Who Should Be Considered a Writer?

That night I slept badly. I dreamed of a white saucepan for milk, with a long handle, and I tried to answer the question: Could it be considered a writer? For some reason I decided that, although it probably shouldn't be considered a writer, it could be admitted into the Writers' Union. I dreamed that there was a session of the selection committee, and a speech by one of the members of the committee to the effect that it was absolutely vital to admit the saucepan, because it was not untalented—at least, so far it hadn't written anything untalented.

"That's true," agreed some important figure thoughtfully, swelling up like a balloon.

•

Of course, a man can dream anything he likes. Even this sort of abracadabra. But such abracadabra can often happen in reality, too. In my time—three terms—as a member of the bureau of the prose section of the Writers' Union, I would hear opinions such as the following one concerning the admission of new members:

"The book which Comrade So-and-so has presented cannot, of course, be called talented. Yes, it's a dull book, but then, we are not a union of *talented* writers, we are a union of *Soviet* writers."

You think that was said as a joke? No, that was asserted seriously, usually by that same sort of Soviet, though untalented, writer.

At first I objected to such a formulation, asserting that the profession of writer is distinguished from all others precisely by the fact that it presupposes the presence of writing talent in its members. I considered that the designation "talented writer" was a tautology. An untalented writer is not a writer at all. I have to admit that back then I even prevented some non-writers from joining the Union, but later on I considered my principle unfair. I saw that 90 percent or more of the members of the Union were non-writers. Which is to say that they cover a certain quantity of paper with a text which is then set in type, printed, bound in a hard or soft cover, and, before being made into pulp, displayed on shop counters. But most of the time this text has no content. Neither moral nor aesthetic, nor even political. I stopped carping at non-writers. I decided that if such non-writers were the overwhelming majority in the Union, then why not accept this one, too, who's not yet a member, but who is in no way worse than those who are. (A hopeless position: a non-writer assumes the duties of a writer and attempts to secure his right to those duties, rather astutely taking advantage of the situation, and later starts to prove that he really is a writer, that only writers like him are needed, and that those defined as writers by the old standards are the real non-writers.)

The above rationale applies only to persons who have not attained some high rank at the time of their entrance into the Writers' Union. But if someone holding a high position joins, they don't say that he should be accepted even though he writes badly. They immediately gabble that he's not just anybody but simply a Great Writer. We shall dwell further on this theme, but now let us return to our respected colleague.

The Legendary Toilet

So then Ivanko came back from America all puffed up. And there was reason to be. He had lived there six years and on holidays did not always return to his native land. Sometimes he vacationed with his family in Nice (have you, reader, ever vacationed in Nice?). Coming home from his distant wanderings, he acquired a car, a new model Volga, in exchange for his work certificates, traded a small two-room apartment for a large three-roomer, furnished it with imported furniture, and equipped it with "their" technology, which included some indescribable toilet which has since become a legend in the literary community.

It would seem a man could want no more. But, as is well-known, a man, especially a creative man, never rests on his accomplishments. He puts in one toilet; then he wants to put in another. But where?

Ah, that's the problem!

Vera Ivanovna Bunina

I was advised to see Vera Ivanovna Bunina. She is director (this should probably be in capitals, too) of the Review Committee in our cooperative. That is, the very committee charged with seeing to it that the board manages its affairs according to the will of the majority of the shareholders and the appropriate legislative body. I dialed her telephone number, hoping to get satisfaction through her from Turganov and his respected protégé, especially since, as they said, she thought very highly of me.

"Well, what do you want?" she asked in a most unfriendly way.

I was slightly taken aback. "What? I want to get an apartment."

"Well, you will, you've been offered Bazhova's apartment."

"I don't want Bazhova's apartment, I want the one that's vacant."

"You mean, you want a good apartment," she said, establishing my guilt immediately.

"Would you want a bad one?" I queried.

"We're not talking about me but about you. Let's speak openly: you want a good apartment." Through her intonation, she emphasized "good," as if in this word the full extent of my downfall was apparent.

"Yes," I was forced to admit, "I want a good apartment."

"So just say so."

"I did."

"Hmm . . ." It looked as if she'd lost her way. She had counted on my arguing that I wanted to get a really bad apartment or, at most, a mediocre one; then she could have objected. But now she was stumped. "Yes, but you're behaving improperly, you're demanding something, you're being difficult . . ."

A Bit about the Bird Troika and Alfred de Musset

Putting down my pipe, I fell to thinking. I began to wonder, Why do these people interpret my every word so negatively? Perhaps I really wasn't conducting myself properly. No, don't think I'm trying to be witty. In the preceding few pages I've tried to produce a certain comic effect, but not here. Here I'm trying to be completely serious. I was confused. I thought that all rights, not only legal, but moral, were so much on my side that I would be given immediate support and that no one would stay on Ivanko's side except Turganov. Well, let's figure they'd get some Kuleshov, too. But take Kozlovsky, for example. Apparently, he doesn't think badly of me, and on the whole, he's not a bad man. Later on they told me (and I knew it myself) that he was a scoundrel, but at that time

I still wasn't sure of it. And that very influential member of the board I mentioned earlier—why had Ivanko become so important to him? An old man, seventy years old, of the former gentry writes about good manners; his wife, who is also of the former gentry, plays the piano. Is it good manners to try to please a bureaucrat? Maybe I really didn't understand something, maybe there were some special circumstances in Ivanko's case, and I was barging ahead, blinded by my craving for expanded living space.

As it happened, I had been in a similar moral dilemma before. In 1970, when the first part of *Chonkin* was being considered by the Writers' Union, the reviewers included not only Gribachev and a certain Vinnichenko, no, they included men with reputations as respectable people. I was even good friends with one of them. But then they got up to speak. Well, Gribachev and Vinnichenko, you know what they said and why. But then one of the respectable ones joined the chorus. He had read the writer under discussion before. He valued his work, but now he couldn't believe his eyes. He was as bitterly disappointed as a refined aesthete like Alfred de Musset must have been when he met obvious coarseness. I sat there, I listened, I thought. Well, it didn't matter about Gribachev and Vinnichenko. But this was a respectable man. And he wasn't speaking through his teeth, he wasn't being forced. He was excited, he was drawing literary parallels, he was speaking *artistically*. I hadn't managed to recover from Alfred de Musset when another one stood up, the one I'd been friends with. He spoke in a hollow voice: he'd known Volodya (to emphasize the former closeness) for a long time. He'd known him as an honest, thinking writer. But you know, Volodya (this directly to me), a writer can and should criticize everything; he can subject any of our shortcomings, any bureaucrat, to the sharpest satire (here he brandished his fist as if with his words he could rout these very shortcomings, this very bureaucrat), but there is one hero who should never be criticized: the people. Even such giants as Saltykov-Shchedrin and Gogol never permitted themselves this. Gogol, who mercilessly ridiculed many shortcomings of old Russia, then wrote "The bird troika! . . ."*

It would have been much easier for me morally if I had thought that they were all scum and scoundrels, but here was a man who had supposedly shared my views. Frankly speaking, I was depressed. Not being very self-assured, I began to have doubts. My friends praised *Chonkin*. But perhaps they praised it out of friendship, afraid to say anything else.

I myself sometimes praise a piece I don't like very much, not wishing to insult a friend. But I also thought all of this looked a little strange. No, I don't claim that my work should appeal to everyone. I had shown it to various people before: some liked it more, some less, some liked it very much, perhaps some (though they didn't tell me, possibly out of politeness) not at all. But here, in the Union, no one liked it, or anything about it. No one liked a single scene, a single line. Both Gribachev and my former oldest friend were agreed on this. It was my friend I thought about and tried to understand, especially since he later assured me that he had been speaking sincerely. I imagined: They ordered him, as a member of the bureau, to read my work. He understands why they gave it to him to read. If, let us suppose, he likes it, then as an honest man (and he does not doubt

* Reference to the last passage of Part One of Gogol's *Dead Souls*, which begins: "And you, Russia, are not you, too, hurtling along like one of those swift troikas nothing can catch?"

his honor) he should say that he likes it. But if he says that, he will bring trouble down upon himself, even expulsion from the bureau. And he has some contracts, books, film scripts, ideas about an award or a prize related to some approaching anniversary. Everything will collapse if he likes this piece. It would be much more convenient for him if this piece turned out to be bad. He starts reading, all the time thinking: Here he's written only one part and right away he sends the manuscript off to the West. He's in a hurry. And all because of some rubbish . . . Why, if he'd at least finished it, there would be something to make a row about. But one part. He says he doesn't know how it ended up over *there.* It wouldn't have if he hadn't wanted it to. He sent it himself and doesn't want to answer for it. He wants to get himself off. He wants me to answer for him. Of course, when you start reading something with ideas like that, you can't possibly like it. But he reads the first line of *Chonkin*: "Now it is impossible to say definitely whether it all really did happen or not . . ." He knits his brow. Why is it impossible to say for sure? And what is this, "whether it all really did happen or not"? If you don't know whether it happened or not, don't bother telling me about it. Then he comes across an unsuccessful line, or even a scene; he gets annoyed and, under the influence of his annoyance, sees only the shortcomings and absolutely none of the merits. After reading it, his mood is completely spoiled. What he read never once elicited either pleasure or a smile. Some of our leftists would figure he thinks that way out of cowardice. But he's no coward. Everyone knows that. In other cases he's defended someone, fought for someone. But when it comes to risking his own neck, he can't just praise a piece he sincerely doesn't like . . .

He comes into the bureau and talks about the bird troika. He speaks with feeling and with total sincerity.

And that is appalling.

"Just wait a little, I will die soon."

Another telephone call. An old woman's voice, breaking into sobs: "Vladimir Nikolaevich, I ask you, please, wait a little, I don't have much time left, I will die soon."

Some stupid practical joke. I hung up. It rang again.

"Vladimir Nikolaevich, I beg of you, don't hang up, hear me out. I understand, you're in a bad situation, you're impatient, but I have cirrhosis of the liver, general arteriosclerosis. I assure you, you won't have long to wait."

I suppose I started to get angry.

"Why are you bothering me?" I said. "Why should I wait for you to die?"

"Vladimir Nikolaevich." I suppose she was getting angry, too. "I was told you are a decent man."

"Well, what of it? Why should I wait for you to die?"

"So you mean you don't want to wait?"

"No, I don't."

"Yes, now I see"—again, tears in her voice—"you are not a decent man. You . . . you . . . you . . ."

This time she hung up.

"Who was that you were talking to so strangely?" my wife asked in surprise.

"Some crazy woman, to hell with her."

The phone again. This time it was a mutual acquaintance of the old woman's and mine. She had called him, sobbing and complaining, and he wanted to know what the problem was, why I had offended her. I explained that I hadn't offended her, I simply hadn't understood why she had called and why I should wait for her to die.

It turned out that Vera Ivanovna Bunina had made a visit to the old woman. After the death of her husband, the old woman had been living alone in a three-room apartment. Vera Ivanovna offered her a one-room apartment in exchange. "Voinovich needs your apartment," she had said.

"My God!" I exclaimed, clutching my forehead. "Why is this Bunina making such a fuss over me? And who is she, anyway? Daughter of *the* Bunin?"*

"No, she's the wife of our Eidlin."

Well, enough! Perhaps it's time to take some action.

The Petition

To: The Board of the Moscow Writers' Housing Cooperative
From: Voinovich, V. N.

STATEMENT

In connection with the fantastic schemes that have arisen regarding apartment 66, which is now vacant, I am obliged to remind the board that it is merely the executive organ of this cooperative and is not empowered to allocate living space at its own discretion.

Being in serious need of improvement in living conditions, unlike other claimants to apartment 66, I categorically insist that this apartment, in accordance with the decision of the general assembly, be granted to me. Any attempts to revoke or amend the decision of the general assembly I shall consider arbitrary and illegal.
February 17, 1973

* Ivan Bunin: the first Russian to win the Nobel Prize for Literature (1933).

"An insolent statement," Kuleshov, a member of the board, told someone.

And Eidlin, Vera Ivanovna Bunina's husband, characterized the statement as gangsterism.

The evaluations of the statement are themselves not very interesting, what I wanted to know was what answer the board would give. But it gave no answer at all.

I waited a day, another, a third—no answer. To arm myself with knowledge, I obtained a copy of the bylaws of the cooperative, which explained that in cases of conflict, upon request of one third of the members of the cooperative, a special meeting of the general assembly may be called within a period of six days.

•

February 22. I composed a new document.

> In accordance with the bylaws of the cooperative, we request that a general assembly of the shareholders be called within a period of six days.

My wife made the rounds of the apartments to gather signatures, which turned out to be easier than for the letter in defense of Sinyavsky and Daniel, but harder than for Solzhenitsyn's invitation to Stockholm. Kozlovsky said that he could not sign because he was a member of the review committee; his colleague N. disappeared and didn't reappear until after the collection of signatures was completed; T. signed, but later asked to scratch her signature, although she was embarrassed and explained her action by the fact that she was about to trade apartments and feared the deal might fall through.

But on the whole they signed gladly. Some out of a sense of justice, others out of regard for the author, still others out of hatred for Turganov and Ivanko. One woman told us that she would sign anything at all against Turganov. I was surprised and asked how our Chairman had injured her. She said that not long ago he had been the chairman of a garage cooperative from which he had been expelled for stealing. They had wanted to bring charges, but then decided that it might lower the respect of the people for the writer's calling. This last surprised me even more, since I hadn't noticed a particularly solicitous attitude toward writers lately. However, I remembered that, on the eve of the trial of Sinyavsky and Daniel, we found out that Kuprianov and company had been keeping a secret den for debauchery. But the affair had been covered up for these same motives: Egorichev, the secretary of the Moscow Municipal Committee at the time, said that the Party should not quarrel with the intelligentsia.

•

February 23. Having gathered about fifty signatures, I took the letter to the secretary of the board, with a copy to Review Committee Chairman Bunina.

It soon became clear that I wasn't the only gangster. Vera Ivanovna Bunina made visits to the signers, cried shame, threatened them, and then demanded by anonymous letter that they remove their signatures. On top of that, she claimed that many signatures were not valid because wives had signed for their husbands, husbands for their wives, and some did not even know what they were signing. That reminded me of earlier campaigns against "petition signers." The same system: blackmail, intimidation of those who signed. Ours was on a lower level, with less possibility of the threats being realized, but still the same thing. By the way, Bunina and Turganov immediately remembered my signatures in defense of the accused, and they brought them up in all subsequent suits to the Regional Executive Committee and the Moscow Soviet.

"But you know that he signed letters in defense of anti-Soviets. But you know that he printed an anti-Soviet story abroad and in general is a well-known anti-Soviet himself."

After such reports, how could a Regional Executive Committee official help but refuse the apartment? After all, he too must be vigilant.

Well, what was I supposed to do? Yield to Sergei Sergeevich? Then most likely I would be called a patriot. That is, until another apartment became available.

The Writer Ivanko

While all this was going on, there were new rumors flying around the courtyard. They said that at Goslitizdat, where our respected colleague, Sergei Sergeevich, is complete master, they are planning to publish a collection of original poetry by our Chairman (some even say that it's in two volumes). A collection of Kozlovsky's poems is also being prepared. And a Chinese novel translated by Eidlin is planned. (I remind you that Eidlin is Vera Ivanovna's husband.) It turns out that this respected family has known Sergei Sergeevich for a long time. Eidlin is a well-known Sinologist. And Sergei Sergeevich is also a Sinologist, Eidlin's student. Besides that, as you remember, Sergei Sergeevich is a personal friend of Nikolai T. Fedorenko. And Nikolai T. Fedorenko is also, besides everything else, a Sinologist. If you look at *Eighteen Poems* by Mao Tse-tung (Moscow, 1957), you will see "Translation edited by N. Fedorenko and L. Eidlin." Small world! The book includes translations by Eidlin and a foreword by Fedorenko. And since we have this volume in hand, I can't resist quoting (please, be patient) one paragraph from the foreword: "Reading the poem 'Liu Pan Chan' in the pages of the journal *Poetry*, one of the heroes of the Chinese War of Liberation told how a small detachment of revolutionary troops engaged a large enemy force. Almost all the soldiers had fallen, and only two or three men were left. Prompted by feelings of loyalty to the Party and the people, they prepared to die. At the last moment, they wished to hear the voice of the Party Central Committee. The radio came on and they heard a recitation of the poem 'Liu Pan Chan.' Oh, what poetry! It excited them, inspiring courage and confidence. The men felt a flood of new strength and decided to break through the encirclement. And they succeeded."

The author of the foreword learned of this episode from an article by the Chinese poet, but imagine what personal delight and love of the Great Pilot he put into his retelling! Straight from the pages of the leading newspaper of the People's Republic of China, *Jên Minh Jih Pao*. But I do not want to distort the facts. I do not think that Nikolai T. Fedorenko ever loved Chairman Mao or his work. Most likely, the passage cited is an example of pure hypocrisy (I invite the author of the foreword to refute my assertion).

We have digressed somewhat. Especially since I do not have sufficient grounds to consider Comrade Fedorenko a participant in his personal friend's battle for the apartment. But since we have touched on this Chinese theme, I will add yet one more stroke to the portrait of our hero, a stroke I had planned to add at the end of my story. As you will see afterward, Ivanko involved important personages in his struggle for a fourth room. His patrons demanded special privileges for him on the grounds that he was a formidable statesman and a formidable writer. The publishing houses made efforts on his behalf, as did someone in the Writers' Union, where he was no longer just a rank-and-file member but was on all the managerial committees (though he had joined only recently). One day I became curious: just what had this writer written? In the Lenin Library, I found out that only one work was registered: *Taiwan: Chinese Land from Time Immemorial,* Moscow, 1955, 44 pp., maps.

From these facts it is difficult to get an idea of the extent of our writer's talent, but one may safely assume that he is no novice when it comes to territorial claims.

Ivanko across the Sea

Let us return to our narrative. However hard Vera Ivanovna Bunina worked in the cornfield discrediting our home-grown signers, they dug their heels in and wouldn't cross off their signatures under any circumstances. One of the board members brought a letter to the Chairman, but Turganov refused to admit either the letter or the board member. He was tired: not only is he Chairman, but he's a human being, too, and a Soviet man, like all Soviet people, has a right to rest. And today is February 23, Soviet Army Day, and tomorrow is Saturday, and the day after tomorrow is Sunday . . .

"Come on the twenty-sixth, on Monday; then we'll look into it."

•

And on the twenty-sixth, a new piece of bad luck: our respected colleague Ivanko suddenly flew off to the United States—as one of my friends said, "to poke around about the copyright convention." Can you imagine the Chairman's position? While he and Vera Ivanovna are here holding the fort, standing to the death, their high-placed protégé is rushing across the Atlantic Ocean to the country of the yellow devil* and he doesn't give the Chairman any help at all. And imagine the position of the protégé himself: here he's flying in this Boeing. Not too bad, of course. Why not dash over to the citadel of imperialism one more time, why not have a good time with that accumulated foreign currency? But while he's off flying, that anti-Soviet, that gangster, that signer is probably breaking into Kuperstock's apartment and arranging his squalid furniture. And what's he supposed to do now? Stay in his three rooms? Without a study? There's even an extra toilet and, pardon me, no place to put it. And our hero's wife, a weak, defenseless woman, is also agitated. Her husband has flown into the very jaws of the shark of imperialism, risking his life, one might say, and now people are talking about some sort of meeting.

Madame Ivanko delivered a request to postpone consideration of their housing question until her husband's return from his business trip abroad.

Could Turganov really refuse a defenseless woman? So he delays.

•

March 2. Turganov convened the board and bitterly informed it that a very unhealthy situation had developed in the cooperative. While our respected colleague Sergei Sergeevich was fulfilling his state assignments, certain persons were gathering signatures and bombarding the board with threatening statements.

Did you get the hint? Certain persons are attempting to disrupt responsible tasks of state, i.e., have come out against the policy of the Party and the government.

* Gorky's anti-American novel is called *City of the Yellow Devil.*

“Just imagine,” said Vera Ivanovna, pursuing this line, “most of the signatures are not those of members of the cooperative but of their relatives! And then, many of them have told me that they didn’t even see what they were signing.”

Naturally, the members of the board were surprised, since several of them had signed the letter themselves.

Despite all this, our Chairman set a general assembly for March 11.

From My Diary

March 5. Our respected colleague returned to his homeland.

Despite difficulties, threatening statements, and anonymous letters, he had honorably fulfilled the Party’s task. It was time to think of arranging his personal life.

•

March 6. I met Galich in the courtyard.

“Did you hear?” he said to me. “Ivanko gave up his claim.”

“Come on!”

“Absolutely. He arrived, found out what kind of scandal there was, and immediately withdrew. You know, he’s a bureaucrat, and if they get him for abuse of power, they can be tough about that sort of thing.”

“They were tough before,” I said, still doubtful. “But perhaps abuse is accepted now?”

“Why, what do you mean? You don’t understand bureaucratic psychology; he would never go near something like that openly. I tell you, he’s withdrawn his claim.”

•

March 7. I told everyone who was interested that Ivanko was no longer my rival.

•

March 8. International Women's Day. I was sitting at home, talking with someone on the phone. The doorbell rang. My neighbor.

"They want you at the office, the board is in session."

I raced down there: would they really hand over the keys?

The high court sat in a small basement room filled with tobacco smoke. There was the Chairman, Vera Ivanovna herself, the other members of the board, and among them, quite modestly, our respected colleague in a knit shirt.

"Vladimir Nikolaevich," Turganov addressed me solemnly, as if it were an occasion of some sort, "we wish to offer you an alternative, which should certainly be acceptable to you. Won't you agree to take the Sadovskys' apartment in your section of the building?"

That apartment again!

"I will not."

"Why not?"

"Because, in the first place, that apartment is only theoretically free, the Sadovskys are not planning to exchange it . . ."

"That's not your problem," Bunina exclaimed.

"In the second place," I said, continuing my objections, "as a member of the cooperative, not as a claimant to apartment 66, I am against Ivanko's getting what is not assigned to him by law."

Our respected colleague leaped up rather unsteadily.

"Bu-u-u-t, why do you think that I want to get more than you?"

And really, why do I think so? He wants to add a room to his apartment and I want to do the same.

"Not only do I not intend to assist your efforts to oblige Comrade Ivanko, on the contrary, I will hinder them in every possible way. The cooperative has a waiting list, those in greater need . . ."

"But you're thinking of yourself!" Again Vera Ivanovna Bunina butted in.

"I wouldn't tell me who to think of if I were you."

"And why do you think," said Turganov, "that you will get Kuperstock's apartment any sooner than the Sadovskys'?"

"Because," I said, "Kuperstock's apartment is vacant and you have no reason to delay transferring it to me."

My statement was perceived as the most extraordinary audacity.

"Show some respect for the Chairman," Turganov demanded. "And respect for the board members."

With this, negotiations were concluded.

They say that, after I left, Ivanko, condemning my intractability, said: "There are hundreds of outrages against the committee every day, but I never protest against them!"

Indeed! Not only is he not embarrassed by his nonresistance to outrages, he actually presents his position as a model of civic honor. And suggests that others follow his example, i.e., not protest against the outrages he perpetrates.*

•

March 10. On the eve of the assembly, the board met once more. For this session I prepared a legal brief which I include in its entirety.

* Ivanko's statement reminds me of a letter from a certain Baptist in the provinces who was harassed by the authorities. The head of the local militia gave utterance to this marvelous notion: "Tolstoy," he said, "was a Baptist, too(!). But he did not resist evil as you do." (V.V.)

A SHORT COMPARATIVE ANALYSIS OF THE RIGHTS OF TWO CLAIMANTS TO AN APARTMENT

(Compiled solely on the basis of law, disregarding moral factors)

IVANKO

1. With a family of three (including himself) has the right to an apartment of $27 + 20 = 47$ square meters. Occupies an apartment of 50.5 square meters. By law, not considered In Need of improvement in living conditions.
2. Wishes to annex to his apartment a room from apartment 66 of 17.5 square meters. $50.5 + 17.5 = 68$ square meters. In this matter, the following statute would apply: "Upon completion of construction of the cooperative building or buildings, each member of the cooperative shall be granted, in perpetuity, and in accordance with the number of shares and the number of members in his family, a separate apartment not to exceed 60 square meters in area." (Housing cooperative bylaws, paragraph 16.)
3. Has been on the waiting list for improvement of living conditions (let us suppose) since October 1972, although it is strange that this was unknown to anyone until now.

VOINOVICH

1. With wife expecting child, has the right to 47 square meters. Occupies a one-room apartment of 24.41 square meters. Is considered Severely in Need of improvement in living conditions.
2. Has been on the waiting list for improvement in living conditions since 1969.
3. The general assembly of January 27 of this year resolved (not recommended, as Turganov maintains) to grant Voinovich the first vacant two-room apartment, which is apartment 66.

SUMMARY

1. In accordance with the decision of the assembly, apartment 66 should be granted to Voinovich.
2. In general, Ivanko has no right to an improvement in living conditions.

"We are afraid of him"

On the evening of March 10, report of victory came through. A friend on the board announced by telephone: "Volodya, if you have something to drink, go ahead. On this occasion you can even allow Irochka a little. By a majority (true, only one vote—four to three), the board voted in your favor. Turganov said, 'Well, if Kuleshov had been here, the result of the vote would have been different.' But we got the main thing: tomorrow the board will report the majority view."

Frankly speaking, what point of view the board was to report interested me very little.

I was sure that the assembly—and it alone is empowered to decide questions of the allocation of living space—would be on my side. There the moral factor would come into play, something my rival mistakenly attaches no importance to.

But on this same March 10, the author of these lines was told of the words of the writer Vorobiev's wife. "We are, of course, behind Voinovich in spirit," she said, "but we will vote as Ivanko wishes because we are afraid of him."

On the morning of March 11, before the assembly, someone suggested to Ivanko that he concede. "No," he said, "I can't yield this apartment to Voinovich. I have this one chance and I won't let it pass."

It seemed he did not doubt that the solution to the question depended solely on his will.

Our Respected Colleague's First Defeat

And now the meeting. Routine matters are discussed: our financial status, plantings in the courtyard, fixing the list of individual housing priority, etc. Finally, they switch to what we actually assembled for. Our Chairman reports: at the last meeting, considering Voinovich's need for improvement of living conditions, following the principle of priority, etc., etc., the assembly decided to grant him the first vacant two-room apartment. Since there is such an apartment now, the board considers that, in execution of the previous decision, it should be granted to Voinovich. Are there any objections?

"Yes!" Our respected competitor raises his hand. He raises it in a rather strange manner, all his fingers bent and only one sticking out in a scornfully limp hook.

"Go ahead." The Chairman's whole look expresses complete sympathy with our respected Sergei Sergeevich.

Our respected colleague explains the matter effortlessly, understanding that it is an empty formality, like a pre-election speech. He has a three-room apartment, but two rooms are adjoining and one is small, and for these reasons he needs another room. Just now there is the possibility of separating a room from apartment 66 and joining it to his apartment. At this point, one comrade stood up and said that he'd been waiting thirteen years for the possibility of improving his living conditions. Why shouldn't Ivanko wait thirteen years, too? What? You're not allowed to break down a main wall? Ivanko has no doubt that he will receive permission to do this. There is an objection that his apartment exceeds the legal norms; the comrades should not worry about that. At the proper levels—an involuntary movement of the finger in the direction of the ceiling—everything will be arranged. The implication: it's only your business to tie up the loose ends and things will be taken care of without you after that.

Our Chairman—the very incarnation of objectivity—calls for a vote: who is for granting the apartment to Voinovich? Who against? For—75; against—3: our respected colleague himself (again holding his index finger in a hook), Bazhova, and another lady who got agitated when she raised her hand "for" and didn't take it down when they voted "against." Turganov jerks up his hand: "I abstain."

After that, there was a little row, which I would not relate if it weren't to add another stroke to the portrait of our hero. Several of those present stood up and expressed their surprise with what had happened. They started saying that some of the board members, the Chairman of the cooperative, and the Director of the Review Committee had behaved very strangely and these people wondered if there shouldn't be new elections at the next assembly. From various quarters there came shouts of "Why at the next one when we can do it now?" From Turganov's point of view a very unhealthy situation was developing. And then Ivanko, our admired and respected colleague, again appeared on the scene and declared that he did not wish to work in such unhealthy circumstances, and announced his resignation from the board.

"I want no part of your squabbles," he said.

There were no tears at this, but applause instead. With a crazed look, cap in hand, the translator Kozlovsky rushed onto the stage. He didn't understand why there was applause, and he considered delight at Sergei Sergeevich's resignation from the board inappropriate, and in protest *he* was leaving the Review Committee. This announcement, too, was greeted with applause. With trembling lips our Chairman rose. They were about to start applauding him, too, but it turned out that they were anticipating things somewhat. He did not want to leave his position, after all. He wanted to remain a figure on the regional level. The comrades, perhaps, did not know that he spent a great deal of time working in the co-operative. He had his red work pass, which would show them his special status. All his activities were recorded there in detail. Next time, he would bring his pass and let them see it. Vladimir Nikolaevich (a low bow in my direction) was worried over nothing. Since such was the will of the assembly, he, the Chairman, was obliged to carry it out and would do so. He would use all his powers to see that their decision was carried out without delay.

With that, the assembly ended. On the way out, I bumped into my defeated rival in the hall. Our admired and respected colleague looked pathetic and dismayed. On his face was nothing but suffering. Of course! He had just had a complete debacle. They didn't just fail to give him what he wanted; they spit in his face, they did not recognize him as a big enough man. And this was strange, too: not one of his minions—not Bunina, not Kuleshov, not Kozlovsky—raised a hand in his defense. Why not? Why, because charity begins at home. They were for their respected colleague only as long as he had the power. As soon as he stumbled, they slunk away. Besides, they are realists, they understand that three or four extra votes don't mean anything. One must hide, bide one's time, and then strike. Whom? That depends on the circumstances: if something happens to our respected colleague, one couldn't find a more dangerous enemy; but if nothing happens to him, his friends will still be his friends.

Thus, Ivanko endured his defeat, and you, reader, probably think this is the end of the whole story. But you see that this is not the last page of our narrative. So, there was something else? What exactly? The permit, a joyful move, and a noisy housewarming? The author would not waste his time and yours on a description of such commonplace personal triumphs. What is described above is only one part of the story. The first part. The second part will be more interesting and it was for its sake that the first part was written.

PART 2

"They'll dance to my tune yet!"

Chronologically, Part 2 begins immediately after Part 1, without any interval. The assembly had just ended. Excited by its results, the shareholders poured out into the courtyard, which was lit with a springtime radiance, and swarmed there in small separate groups, considering the events that had occurred from various sides. Nor did our respected colleague hurry home. He stood in the middle of the courtyard, surrounded by his minions. Putting his hands behind his back and shaking his right leg, he said loudly, wishing to be heard by all, "Never mind, I'll fix their wagon. They'll dance to my tune yet."

"They," as you must realize, are the tenants of our building, the shareholders of the Moscow Writers' Housing Cooperative. That is a rather large group of people, which, when necessary, is called a collective. Under our system, the collective is practically the holy of holies. If the assembly had been on Ivanko's side, he would certainly have used it in his future efforts. He would lean on the opinion of the collective, he would hoist up the authority of the collective, he would call for respect for the collective. But the collective, since it voted against him, was no longer a collective, but a "they" which he intended to turn into a song-and-dance group.

The aforementioned words of Ivanko immediately spread around the courtyard and reached the ears of the author of these notes. But, being in a state of understandably good humor, that author did not attach any significance to his words. What does it matter what a man says when he's hot under the collar . . .

A Meeting with a Prophet

As it happened, on this same day, March 11, there was fine sunny weather. And the author of this work decided to take a walk in the sun. In the courtyard he met the very same shareholder who had predicted at the beginning of our story (do you remember?), "You will get the apartment, but with very great difficulty."

"You are a wise man and practically a prophet," said the author on meeting this shareholder. "Explain to me, please, what our respected colleague was counting on? After all, they say he's not stupid. He must have understood that he had nothing to hope for from the sympathy of the assembly."

"You are mistaken!" the author's interlocutor objected hotly. "He can't understand anything. He is used to having assemblies conducted according to prearranged plans. Everything is decided in the preparatory stage and the assembly is simply a ceremonial display: it accepts, enacts, supports, approves. However, the struggle isn't over for him. If you agree that I am a prophet, note yet another of my predictions. Ivanko's saying that we'll all dance to his tune is by no means an idle threat. He'll still spoil things for you, you'll see."

Good Advice

He must have been looking in a crystal ball.

A few days passed and in the courtyard I met . . . who do you think? Kozlovsky, of course.

"Listen, old man," he said into my left ear, "you know where I've been?"

"Well, come on, don't torture me, finish me off right away."

"Old man, I was at Melentiev's."*

"You know such important people? You saw Melentiev in the flesh? Let me touch you."

"Hands off, old man, I'm ticklish. You know what Melentiev said? He said, 'Tell Voinovich there's no way he'll get this apartment.' "

"Oh, God! Melentiev himself! Just up and said, 'Tell Voinovich? . . .' That means he knows that I exist! Melentiev himself . . . Such a big man!"

Kozlovsky was distressed. "Old man, I see that you're not a very serious person. Take some good advice: don't play the fool, agree to take Bazhova's apartment while they're still offering it. Or here's what. You know what I would do in your position? In your position," he became animated, as if something had suddenly dawned on him, "I would call Ivanko."

"And in your position, you know what I would do? To start, I would stop toadying to Ivanko!"

"So that's how it is! Well, look . . . I've said everything I have to say to you."

Later he told someone, "They say I'm Ivanko's lackey. Well, I don't need Ivanko, I have the famous Rasul Gamzatov."

One man who ran into Kozlovsky asked him, "Yashka, why are you working so diligently against Voinovich? When it was a question of the apartment Lipatov got, you called up everyone and said Voinovich was a marvelous writer† and that if we didn't give the apartment to him, you would write a letter to the procurator general."

* Yuri Melentiev: now Minister of Culture of the RSFSR; at the time of *The Ivankiad,* an influential publisher and literary bureaucrat.

† It is awkward for me to repeat this epithet, but I don't do it out of boastfulness, only to characterize Kozlovsky. (V.V.)

"Yes, I said that because I wanted to spite Vorobikha . . ."

New Figures

A few more days passed, and this same Kozlovsky spread a new rumor around the courtyard. Chairman Stukalin of the State Committee on Publishing wrote a letter to the Mayor of Moscow, Chairman Promyslov of the Moscow Soviet, and the latter has issued a resolution favorable to Ivanko. There will be a new assembly, at which Simonov will speak in Ivanko's favor. Simonov is on vacation in the Crimea, but will certainly return in time for the assembly. Imagine, such figures brought into play! This is no longer just on a regional level, it's even higher. If things develop any further in the same direction, there's no telling what summits we might reach.

Read the Classics

Two weeks had passed since the assembly, every day more and more ominous rumors were being spread, and apartment 66 was sealed up. I went to look at it: there was a strip of paper stuck to the door with the round seal of the building management on it. This piece of paper had no legal force, but considering the general deference toward seals, it was better not to touch it. Two weeks had passed, they were saying that Klenov-Kuperstock had already taken an apartment in Israel with a view of the Wailing Wall; and what was going on here? Why didn't they give me the keys, why didn't they hand me the permit? There might even be a short notice of our achievement in the newspaper: here, yet another family had celebrated their housewarming. But they didn't give us the permit, because the decision of the assembly had not been confirmed by the Regional Executive Committee. The Regional Executive Committee might have been happy to confirm it (they were not, as we will see), but they had nothing to confirm; the documents had not yet been submitted. Why hadn't they been submitted? How could I find out? Aha, there he was, the Chairman in person, moving across the courtyard with a large briefcase under his arm. He moved his feet most democratically, just like a simple mortal, and—you just won't believe it—he had no escort. One could approach him without ceremony.

"Boris Alexandrovich, what's going on? Can it be that the documents haven't been processed yet?"

Boris Alexandrovich started to tremble with righteous indignation. No, not in reaction to the importunate petitioner, but in reaction to the negligent workers of the building management.

"You've got to understand, copying documents requires a typewriter with a large carriage, and they can't get one of those typewriters. Just unbelievable! And then everyone jumps on the Chairman. The Chairman is to blame for everything, according to them. The Chairman should even get them the typewriter. They can't do it themselves."

Let us look into the Chairman's eyes. What do we see, behind those glasses? No, apparently everything is all right. As the poet said:

. . . No lies are in his look.
His eyes truthfully proclaim
Their master as a crook.

Actually, I'm not a cunning person. At least I don't seem so to myself. But.

Luckily for me, I had been rereading Pushkin's *Dubrovsky* the night before to calm myself. And I got to the part where Assessor Shabashkin sends Andrei Gavrilovich "an invitation to deliver immediately an explanation concerning his ownership of the village of Kistenevka." As we know, the old man, sure of his rights, answered with a rather rude letter. It would seem that Shabashkin should have been offended. Oh, no. "This letter made a very pleasant impression upon Assessor Shabashkin's soul. He realized (1) that Dubrovsky had no sense for business and (2) that it would not be difficult to place such a hot-tempered and imprudent man in a most disadvantageous position."

Reading this passage, I was astounded at how similar this situation was to our story. And I began to think that I had fallen into old man Dubrovsky's position because my character was the same as his. First, I have little sense for business; and second, I am excitable and imprudent. On top of that, I have not one but a whole gang of Shabashkins working against me. And I thought: Literature should teach us something. I should learn at least one practical lesson. No, Messrs. Shabashkin, I will try not to repeat Andrei Gavrilovich's mistakes. I will be restrained and cool. I will not act on my first impulse. I will act with circumspection and calculation, and if you choose cunning as your weapon, I will be more cunning than you.

"Boris Alexandrovich," I said, "as you know, when Klenov moved, he left the maintenance and construction department money for the apartment's repair, as he was supposed to."

"Yes, yes." The Chairman nodded his head in agreement.

"So, while your subordinates are looking for a typewriter with a large carriage, why should the apartment just sit there? It seems to me, regardless of who gets it, you should apply to the maintenance department and have them send over workmen to begin the repairs."

"I do not deal with such questions," the Chairman said squeamishly. "The building manager deals with them."

Really, how could I have thought that he, the Chairman, would stoop to such trifles?

Colonel Emyshev

Let's take a look in the office. Sitting at his desk is Building Manager Mikhail Fedorovich Emyshev, a Communist since 1932. Sometimes he says since '31, sometimes since '33, but with such a long service record, you could easily lose track. I address him by name and patronymic. I explain: a typewriter with a large carriage . . . Klenov . . . money . . . maintenance and construction department. Instead of answering, he starts reeling off his biography in condensed form:

"You understand, Vladimir, I am a colonel. I have a pension of two hundred rubles. I don't need these problems of yours. Who does? I always earn my hundred and twenty rubles excluding pension. I've been a member of the Party since '31 . . ."

That is, of course, very commendable, but I remind him again of the purpose of my visit. Money . . . Klenov . . . maintenance and construction department. He knits his brow: there I go again with my trifles.

"But you understand, I am a colonel . . ."

"I understand, Mikhail Fedorovich, I appreciate that. We must cherish the martial glory of our fathers, but I've come to you now concerning the maintenance and construction department. The thing is that when Klenov moved he paid for the repair of the apartment, so shouldn't we call over there and have them send some workers?"

"No, you do not understand me . . ."

"I understand, I understand. I can just see you with three stars on your epaulettes, beneath the flag singed by the flames of battle . . . Don't your old wounds ache before it rains?"

"What?"

"I'm still on the repairs. You probably have an order for them. Open that drawer there. There it is, the order, that's it. I understand, memories of the war crowded into your mind, your sight was dimmed, it would be nice to get drunk, but what can you do, since the Party has entrusted you with this high post, you have to work."

The ex-colonel tarries, not knowing what to do. Peaceful workdays are sometimes rougher than fierce battles. He gets the order out of the drawer, puts it on the desk, then back in the drawer, then back on the desk, and dials Turganov's telephone number. No answer.

"You understand," sighs the building manager, "I really earn my hundred and twenty rubles."

"Just as it should be," I agree, "but earn them here first. Give me the order . . . Let go, or we'll tear the document. So, what should we check? The order number, the account number, the telephone number, the address of the office. That's it. Now I'll go to the office and arrange the repairs. So long!"

This time I didn't manage to hear our building manager's glorious biography to the end.

A Sneaky Scheme

Do you understand why I was so concerned about the repairs? Well, in the first place, of course, so that something would get done while we were waiting. In the second place, I had worked out a strategic plan which will become clear to you later on.

I shall not describe my misadventures at the maintenance and construction department, everyone knows what that's like. First the order was mislaid, then it turned out that only one painter did primers, and he wasn't there, he was working somewhere on Gorky Street and they didn't know how much longer he would be—maybe a week, maybe a month.

"Wait," they said.

Well, it wouldn't be the first time we waited, but time, as they say, waits for no man. The rumors got more alarming every day. People didn't seem to talk about anything else around the courtyard but this squabble over the apartments. One heard only: Stukalin, Promyslov, Melentiev, Ivanko . . . yes, and sometimes my name was mentioned in that distinguished company.

Members of the board, well disposed toward me, advised me to drop in on Ilin.

"What's Ilin got to do with it?" I asked. "Why can't you speak up yourselves?"

Again they looked at me as if I weren't normal. "Don't you understand?"

I didn't understand.

But there was nothing I could do. I had hoped I would never step across that threshold again, and now . . .

General Ilin

So, we present to the reader yet another participant in our drama. Ilin, Viktor Nikolaevich, Executive Secretary of the Moscow branch of the Writers' Union, Lieutenant-General of State Security, cultural worker emeritus of the RSFSR, veteran of the Patriotic War. He saw service in the various police and intelligence "organs" of the U.S.S.R., and he had medals, an honorary pistol, and ten years in prison (according to him, he refused to give evidence against a friend). Long-standing service in the area of culture.

"I've been working with writers since '24," he says.

Now, like the majority of workers in the punitive services, he is sentimental.

"Did you hear: Igor Chekin died, my exact contemporary. It's our generation's turn. As Olesha said: Shells are bursting somewhere close." And behind his gold-framed glasses there is a meager, manly tear.

Sometimes he brings out a yellowed photograph of two kids with bows in their hair: that's how he left them, when he went *there*. He might not have had to leave them if he had agreed to become a traitor. Strangely enough, he brings up this story when he's wringing a confession from his victim.

"If you were an honorable man, you would say who gave you this letter to sign." But he immediately retreats. "No, no, I'm not pressuring you." And after a bit he completely reverses himself. "Look, I'm not asking who gave you this letter to sign."

Once I played up to him and said, "Viktor Nikolaevich, in your time there was someone you thought was innocent and you even suffered for him."

"But he was my friend," he said, agitated. "I knew him well."

With those he did not know sufficiently well, he acted differently.

They say he behaved decently in the camps. After his release, he worked somewhere on construction projects, and then returned to work with the writers. He gladly fulfills everyday requests. If you need to have a telephone installed, to place a relative in a hospital, to join a garage cooperative, or to get a spot in the cemetery, go to him. He'll call whomever he has to and write an explanatory letter (he knows about those things). But if they order him to kill you, he will.

"I've always been true to the Party, and will be till I die." Those are his words.

His notions of literature are quite primitive, and he doesn't pretend to be a connoisseur. But when it comes to the investigation department, he is a professional (and I think that is the greatest compliment he could ever want). He barely sticks to the formalities of his investigative responsibilities. He thinks up new tricks to cunningly lure you into a trap, to make use of your mistakes. He plays with you, as a sated cat plays with a mouse, and not just the result, but the very procedure of the game is important. He may have no hostility toward you or may even sympathize with you; but that has no significance and is in no way reflected in his actions toward you. He has his good points. You can scream at him and he won't be offended (though in the interests of the case he may pretend he is offended); you can flatter him and he won't believe it. He is a bit of an actor, too, and his behavior toward you at a given moment means nothing. And if he walks past you without saying hello or, on the contrary, throws himself into your arms, don't pay any attention, he simply wants to give you a certain impression. In reality, his not saying hello doesn't mean he's angry with you, and his embracing you doesn't mean he loves you. But the main impression he wants to create at all times is that nowadays, when ideals are not so high, maybe he's being an eccentric, but he serves the Party and only it, and for its sake he is ready to sit in the office of the Secretary of the Writers' Union—or in a prison cell. They say he keeps his word. That is not entirely true. Keeping his word is not always part of his plans, not always within his power. The specific character of his work keeps him from not making empty promises, but when he has promised something, and is able to do it and does it, he is obviously pleased and happily accepts expressions of gratitude.

Memories . . .

So, Ilin's office.

Since 1968, the year part of *Chonkin* was sent to the West to be published, it had been repeatedly explained to me in this office that I had placed my pen at the service of some sort of intelligence agency and of international reactionaries. This was the place where I was reminded of a pronouncement by the founder of socialist realism: "If the enemy does not surrender, he is destroyed." Here I was interrogated by the owner of the office himself, by the commission set up to investigate my activities (I should be proud, not everyone is given such an honor), by the secretariat in full strength. Here were enacted (and are enacted even now) scenes worthy of the pen of Kafka and Orwell. Here the writer Telpugov said of *Chonkin:*

"This job should not be handled by us but by the appropriate organs. I myself shall petition at all levels for the author's punishment. It is unimportant how it got abroad. If it hadn't gotten anywhere, but had just been written and was lying in a desk drawer . . . Even if it hadn't been written, but just conceived . . ."

That's how much my simple idea terrified him. But his own idea of putting a man in prison for merely conceiving a work, perhaps a bad one but one not even written, did not terrify any of the witnesses of this conversation. On the contrary, they nodded their heads yes, quite true.

. . . and Reflections

I often wondered why there were so many former (and not just former) punitive-service employees in the Writers' Union. And now I understand: because they really are writers. How many plots they've created, complete fabrications! And such plots! Subversive organizations spreading across the whole country. Numerous ties with foreign intelligence services. With Fascists, Trotskyites, Zionists, and other groups. Portable transmitters, silent pistols, suitcases with false bottoms, codes, secret meetings, addresses, foreign currency, sex, pornography, stabs in the back, bribery, blackmail, potassium cyanide, sabotage, and provocation . . . How much of all this did they make up themselves, the unsung investigators of the appropriate organs! Take for example the now famous shorthand report of the trial of Bukharin et al. Don't regard it as a document, for it is not a document; don't think about methods of investigation, about why Krestinsky first offered one story, then the others. Regard it as a work of art. And you will agree that you've never read anything like it in all of world literature. What well-defined characters! What a grandiose plot, and how cohesive and integrated everything was. It's just too bad that the characters were living people, otherwise you might be able to stand reading it.

In the Office

Ilin greeted me suspiciously, offered me a chair, but did not extend his hand. And it wasn't surprising. Korzhavin* had just been there. He had asked for a reference for an exit visa to Israel. Perhaps I had come for the same thing.

* Naum Korzhavin: poet, emigrated from the Soviet Union in 1974.

But once he learned that it was merely a matter of an apartment, he beamed and started using the familiar "thou" with me as a sign of complete sympathy.

"Well, what are you worried about?" he said. "The assembly decided in your favor, that means everything's all right. Well, of course it's possible that Melentiev will take advantage of his connections and support Ivanko, but they won't get anywhere with that. Who is this Turganov? A Ukrainian translator? Oh, come on. There's nothing to worry about. When they deny your request, we'll go to the Regional Executive Committee."

Then he complained that I wasn't very close to the organization and sent greetings to my wife, telling me to reassure her.

"In her condition," he said, "she shouldn't let herself worry."

A Telephone Conversation

If Chairman Turganov, like President Nixon, were forced to submit tapes of recorded conversations concerning apartment 66, we should certainly discover among them one of a conversation which took place on April 3, 1973, between the Chairman and the author of these lines. Here is a record, not verbatim, but fairly close.

"Boris Alexandrovich, I hear that tomorrow the Regional Executive Committee is going to approve the minutes of the March 11 assembly."

"Yes, yes."

"That means the matter of my apartment will also be approved then?"

"No, that matter will not be decided tomorrow. It will be investigated separately."

"Why separately?"

"I have not been informed."

"Boris Alexandrovich, please excuse me if it is not so, but it appears to me that you have forgotten your promise and are involved in intrigues again."

"Vladimir Nikolaevich, I will not permit you to speak to me in that tone of voice."

"Boris Alexandrovich, it is difficult for me to speak to you in any other tone. It seems strange to me that you, who do not consider yourself a stupid man, won't understand that in the end they'll just run you out of offi—"

Break in the conversation, rapid beeps: *tu-tu-tu-tu.*

A tape recorder is nice because it preserves not only the words but the intonation, too, which sometimes intensifies and reinforces what is said, and sometimes gives the words an opposite meaning. On the tape we've just heard, there are two basic intonations, first malevolence changing to exultation, then righteous indignation.

Inspector Budarin

Now let us go to the Regional Cooperative Inspector, Comrade Budarin. Of course, he will tell us this is not a visiting day and that information cannot be given out. But if we show a little persistence . . .

"No, tomorrow other matters will be investigated. Not yours."

Comrade Promyslov's Instructions

Nevertheless, the next day, April 4, the writer of these lines decided to visit the Regional Executive Committee personally and satisfy himself that this matter would not be considered. And so there were three of us: the building manager, Emyshev, one of the board members, and your humble servant.

On the way, the building manager, recognizing in me an eager listener, began to talk. "You understand . . . What's your name . . . Vladimir, right? You understand, I've been a member of the Party since '32, I'm a colonel. I have medals down to there [he moves his hand down past his waist]. I have a pension of two hundred rubles. And here I get a hundred and twenty. But I always earn that money. Why should I mess around with this? As far as I'm concerned, you can all live in five-room apartments. I'm a colonel . . ."

We arrived at the Executive Committee. We are told we must wait a bit. We waited.

"You understand," the building manager reproaches me, "they say I'm Turganov's buddy. But I'm not his buddy. I'm a colonel. I have a pension of two hundred rubles. I worked in the Scientific Research Institute as deputy director. The director was Academician Yudaev, and I was the deputy. But then I had to leave. They paid me a hundred and twenty and later added sixty more. I had to leave."

"Why?" I asked, surprised. "It was good that they paid you more."

"Not really, you understand, Vladimir. I'm a colonel. I have a pension of two hundred rubles. And I can get a hundred and twenty more."

"Well?"

"You don't understand," grieved the building manager. "I've been a member of the Party since '31. That means they'll pay me a pension of a hundred and twenty, but Party dues take a hundred and eighty all together."

"How wonderful!" I said.

"What's so wonderful?" said the former colonel, perplexed. "I tell you they pay a hundred and twenty and take a hundred and eighty."

"That's it precisely. That's what I'm talking about. You have a real opportunity to help the Party, to thank it for all it has done for you, for bringing you from the bottom . . . It was from the bottom, wasn't it?"

"Well!"

"The Party brought you up from the bottom to such heights, and you grudge paying a few rubles back. I never expected that from you, Mikhail Fedorovich. If you were a young Communist—but with a service record like yours . . ."

I did not manage to convince my companion, because Inspector Budarin appeared and invited the building manager and the board member to the meeting.

As an unauthorized person, I stayed outside. I walked up and down the hall, thinking. How can they refuse, if they have no grounds? What could they think up?

The board member came out, and by his face I could immediately tell—they had refused.

"They didn't refuse," he said, "they shelved it."

It turned out that Kozlovsky hadn't been lying: they really did have a letter from Stukalin and instructions from Promyslov. I don't know what was in Stukalin's letter, although the building manager did say it listed Ivanko's services. Promyslov's instructions were much shorter and so they could be passed on to me verbatim: "Please consider this and help him." The Regional Executive Committee was in a desperate situation.

"We have no grounds to refuse Voinovich, but we can't brush aside Promyslov's instructions."

The situation really did look desperate. They can't refuse Voinovich, they can't satisfy Ivanko, and they can't brush aside Promyslov.

"But isn't it possible," I asked in my simplicity, "not to brush Promyslov aside, but to write him politely that there is no way to grant his request, because . . ."

They look at me as if I'm an idiot. Even worse, as if I were some kind of evil-minded character. Could one really answer Comrade Promyslov himself like that? And, apparently, Comrade Ivanko is a prominent personage, too. Every day there are calls from some place. From the Planet Press, from the Torch Press, and some Pirogov called from the City Committee.

"Hint that you're not Jewish."

Do you understand what's happening? On one side, our respected colleague Sergei Sergeevich Ivanko, prominent statesman and writer, and on the other side, some Voinovich person, the husband of a pregnant woman.

But what's interesting is that it's not just my opponents but my supporters as well who talk that way. They're always telling me, "Calm down, calm down, you do everything wrong, you only get in our way, you'd better shut up."

They think everything should be done on the sly. One should fight with Chairman Turganov, but under no circumstances touch Ivanko. One should only bow and scrape before Ivanko.

"Of course, we understand that our respected colleague Sergei Sergeevich needs it very much, and we would gladly . . . but . . ."

And then follows the argument that Voinovich's wife is in her nth month.

Once I got angry. "Why do you defend me so strangely, anyway? Why don't you say that as far as you're concerned I'm not just a nobody, I'm a writer?"

They look at me and throw up their hands. Is he crazy? He doesn't understand. As if to defend me on principle were to testify to one's own unreliability. Why? After all, I have not been deprived of my civil rights, I have not been expelled from the Writers' Union, two of my books had just been published at the same time (one even at Politizdat, which is in itself a sign of loyalty). But despite all this, they can't use a single argument in my defense except my pregnant wife.

Our respected colleague's supporters are not restrained in their eloquence. Ivanko is a prominent statesman, a prominent writer. Voinovich is an anti-Soviet, a signer, a corrupt person, a Jew (true, this last they do not say outright, but they allude to it rather transparently). My supporters seem not to hear all this.

"Yes, but you understand, his wife is expecting."

I wrote a letter to some office; I showed it to one of my well-wishers and saw that he was not pleased.

"Why do you write in a demanding tone? Request. Tell them you're from the working class, that you wrote a song about the cosmonauts, write them that your wife is expecting, and, I feel awkward saying this to you, hint to them somehow that you're not Jewish."

I got furious.

"Why should I beg someone for my own apartment? I don't want to write that I'm from the working class, I don't want to write about the cosmonauts, I don't want to write that I'm not Jewish. I want to get the apartment regardless of whether I signed some letter or wrote some ideologically acceptable work."

"Well, you see, we sincerely want to help you, but you ruin everything for us. In the end, is it the principle or the apartment that's important to you?"

(Only one man agreed that the principle was also important, but of him later.)

Nevertheless, if even one member of the board had definitely declared that Ivanko's claims were illegal and could not be satisfied, I am sure that this whole affair would never have occurred (true, I would also have lost a great wealth of factual material for my story).

Where Was Solzhenitsyn Published?

Here's what I think. By accepting the rules of the game foisted upon us by the Turganovs and Ivankos, don't we contribute to their tyranny over many areas of our life?

Here's what people told me: Writer X was at a reception at the apartment of a candidate-member of the Politburo. To the candidate's question of how things were in literature, he said things were pretty bad. How so? The writer tried to explain a few things. The candidate was extremely surprised. So many writers visited him, but why didn't they ever say anything like that?

Of course, the candidate-member could have figured things out for himself, but really no one told him anything. (Usually they said that, on the whole, everything was fine, or even wonderful, and that conditions for writers in our country were like nowhere else. But there were isolated imperfections—for example, the guest's book had yet to get published.)

Here's what an admirer of Solzhenitsyn told me. The same night that his beloved writer was arrested, the narrator was riding in a taxi along the Sadovoe Ring Road with a few colleagues. Learning that his passengers were writers, the driver started asking about Solzhenitsyn. The passengers very much wanted to enlighten the ordinary reader.

"But," the narrator told me, "we couldn't tell him straight out. We hinted. I said, 'Solzhenitsyn? Yes, there is such a writer. Where was he published? I couldn't say exactly.' I turned to one of my companions. 'Do you remember where Solzhenitsyn was published? Some journal, I suppose.' He also made a troubled face, knit his brows. 'Yes, in *Novy Mir*, I think.' "

The admirer of Solzhenitsyn clearly expected my approval. I said, "Why couldn't you have said what you knew without any personal evaluation at all? That Solzhenitsyn was published in *Novy Mir*, that *Ivan Denisovich* came out in a magazine and also as a separate book and was nominated for a Lenin Prize?"

"How could I do that?"

"Why not? It was no threat to you. You abuse someone who prints a fraudulent article in a newspaper, but what do you do yourself? From what you said, the driver could have come to only one conclusion: Solzhenitsyn is completely unknown, even the writers do not know for sure what he wrote and where he was published. It would have been better if you hadn't told him anything."

The Directive Rainbow

So, what's going on? If we call the affair by its true name, what's going on is the purest sort of criminal activity. One man promises a bribe to persons who will help him expand his apartment illegally, and these in turn try to bribe him to get their works published. But, whereas usually only the one giving the bribe has a material gain, in this case, with the mutual exchange of bribes, everyone ends up with a profit. This is because Ivanko offers a bribe from the state's pocket, and, in exchange, his contractors slip him an apartment which they don't even own. In our country, bribery is considered one of the most serious crimes, one for which the death penalty is given fairly often. Who isn't accused of bribery? Feofanov, for example, in one of his satirical articles insisted that a ten-ruble note accepted by a salesgirl for goods sold on the side was a bribe. But that salesgirl took the tenner in secret. She was afraid. But these people aren't afraid of anybody. They don't hide what they do, or why, or how, from anybody. Everything goes on in full sight of the community, and not just any community, but the writers' community. Where any one of us could write about it. Several well-known satirists live in our building. The great Lench himself lives in our building. And wouldn't a satirical article in *Krokodil* get them mad! what a bang it would make. But maybe those big chiefs who stuck up for our respected colleague, and in that way assisted in the commission of the crime, were not sufficiently well informed? Let us try to imagine how that could have happened. Let's suppose our respected colleague went to the minister and explained his position. So that's it, he says, there's an opportunity to improve my housing conditions; some free space turned up in the building and the leaders of the cooperative aren't against it, but I need a petition from my place of employment. The minister knows our respected colleague as an excellent worker and highly values his literary talent (he'd read his work *Taiwan: Chinese Land from Time Immemorial* many times and with great enjoyment). In that case, why not grant such a trifling request? Especially since Yuri Serafimovich Melentiev is also supporting him.

"Well," says the minister, "compose a letter and I'll sign it."

Now let us try to put ourselves in Comrade Promyslov's position. He receives a letter. The letter is not from just anybody but from the minister. The minister has a quite trivial request. A valuable worker, a member of the CPSU, a member of the board of the city committee, the writer Ivanko needs all of 1 (one) room of seventeen and a half square meters. That's all? It's ridiculous to think what a room of seventeen and a half square meters means to Promyslov. To him, the mayor of one of the largest cities in the world containing millions of rooms with a total area of tens of millions of square meters. And especially with the present scale of housing construction. And the minister is asking for all of . . . For heaven's sake, go ahead! And the mayor of one of the largest cities in the world writes, "Please consider this and help him." He doesn't go into detail. For the details, there are lower-ranking comrades. True, experts say that this statement meant nothing, it was just a formal reply. You can't just say no to a minister, and so Promyslov wrote, "Please consider this and help him." If he'd taken a more energetic position, he would have written more categorically, for example, "Look into this matter and report to me!" And he would have put a big exclamation point at the end. "Help" means: depending on circumstances.

Other experts say it's not the text that's important but the color of the pencil. A statement in red pencil means an order, in blue a formal reply. But let's put ourselves in the position of the lower-ranking comrade. Maybe he's color-blind, or maybe he doesn't remember exactly what color a directive is, but, just in case, he'll obey all the colors of the rainbow.

From the Author's Epistolary Storehouse

"I can't say anything about Promyslov, but Stukalin is a very decent man," one of the leading engineers of the human soul assured the author of these lines. "Of course, he didn't know the real situation. Ivanko took advantage of the fact that, unfortunately, Boris Ivanovich is too soft and credulous."

That's all right, credulity is the very shortcoming that even the founder of our scientific view of the world regarded indulgently. But, in that case, shouldn't we open the eyes of the credulous Boris Ivanovich to one of his closest comrades-in-arms?

Below, the author offers the reader two examples of his epistolary style.

April 5, 1973

Comrade Stukalin, Boris Ivanovich
Chairman of the State Committee
on Publishing, Polygraphy, and
the Book Trade of the Council
of Ministers of the U.S.S.R.

Dear Boris Ivanovich:
When you requested the Chairman of the Moscow Soviet to help your colleague Ivanko, you were, perhaps, unaware of the real state of affairs. It is as follows . . . [The state of affairs is explained.]

. . . Having no legal grounds for the expansion of his apartment, Ivanko is attempting to attain his goal by illegal means. His impudence and unscrupulousness are truly surprising. Here are just a few facts.

As a member of the board of the cooperative, he actively pushed his own candidature at the board meetings, which is unethical in itself (members of the board don't participate in discussions of their own housing problems).

To the question of one of the members of the board as

to whether he would not feel uncomfortable in a luxurious four-room apartment, knowing that his comrade, a writer, was huddled with his wife and child in one room, Ivanko replied: "Well, I'd manage to get over it."

At the next session of the board, in answer to my objections, he said, "There are hundreds of outrages against the committee every day and I never protest against them."

When Ivanko's claims were rejected at the assembly, he resigned from the board in protest and, after the assembly, announced for all to hear, "I'll fix their wagon. They'll dance to my tune yet."

Rumors of Ivanko's omnipotence and invulnerability spread among the tenants of our building. They say he can cut any book from the publication plan and can decrease or increase an edition at his own discretion. Maybe Ivanko himself has nothing to do with these rumors. But then what is he counting on? The thing is that Ivanko's official position is the single chief trump in his unscrupulous and dirty fight.

This is, Boris Ivanovich, an unlovely and, what is more, a scandalous affair. Ivanko's behavior angers not only me and not only the members of our cooperative; it angers the writers' community. I hope that your protection of Ivanko is explicable solely by your lack of information.

I hope also that the leadership and the Party organization will investigate this matter objectively and give this brazen extortioner his just deserts.

I shall await your reply within the two-week period set by the edict of the Presidium of the Supreme Soviet of the U.S.S.R., "On the Review Procedure for Workers' Applications and Complaints."

Respectfully,
Vladimir Voinovich

April 8, 1973

Comrade Verchenko, Yuri Nikolaevich
Secretary of the Writers' Union
of the U.S.S.R.

Dear Yuri Nikolaevich:

I am sending you a copy of my letter to the Chairman of the State Committee on Publishing, Polygraphy, and the Book Trade of the Council of Ministers of the U.S.S.R.

S. S. Ivanko, of whom I speak in that letter, though only recently admitted to the Writers' Union, is already a member of various bureaus, commissions, and panels. I believe that the facts I have set forth give us reason to fear that Ivanko may take advantage of his social position, as he has of his official one, for mercenary goals.

I ask the Secretariat of the Writers' Union of the U.S.S.R. and you, personally, to take notice of and evaluate Comrade Ivanko's activities.

Respectfully,
Vladimir Voinovich

I sent a second copy (forgive me, stern reader) to Party Organization Secretary of the State Committee on Publishing Soloviov.

Event on a Sunny Day

The sun wakes Sergei Sergeevich. It shines right through the thin curtain into his eyes. God, has he really overslept, is he late for work? The alarm clock sitting on the chair next to the bed reassures him. No, it looks like everything's all right. But what's the sun doing up so early? He moves his eyes from the alarm clock to the calendar and sees it is already the middle of April, which means the days are getting longer. All natural phenomena can be explained so easily. Insignificant quantitative changes become qualitative—a normal law of dialectics. But if you investigate them, qualitative changes also become quantitative. That's not a bad idea; it should be noted down. Who knows, maybe it'll come in handy for his new book. After all, he is a writer and a writer must write books; in the end that's his duty and his responsibility.

At breakfast he shares the new idea with his wife, and she is delighted: how original and how profound. Yet, at the same time, she is very upset.

"It's terrible," she says, "that you have nowhere to work. I can't wait until we get that fourth room so we can set up a study for you."

"No," he objects, "not one word about a study. I want that room to be your boudoir." He is embarrassed, and snickers pronouncing that non-Russian word.

His wife displays unusual persistence, and they squabble a bit, but the conflict does not spoil his mood since it is a conflict between something wonderful and something even more splendid.

"But don't you think," his wife asks, "that we're counting our chickens, that that scoundrel with the pregnant wife will get the whole cooperative against us and that they'll vote 'no' again?"

Sergei Sergeevich frowns. Frankly speaking, the fear his wife expressed troubles him as well. He has thought a great deal about his competitor. "He's a strange man," thinks Sergei Sergeevich. "Why is he so stubborn? Hasn't he understood yet that I am an important person, maybe even a very important person? He has a beautiful private one-room apartment. Is that really so little for an unimportant person? During the war people lived in much worse conditions. And even now our heroic youth at shock construction sites live in dugouts, in tents, and so what, they can take it . . ."

"You don't have to worry," he says to his wife. "With our connections it won't be difficult to settle this matter."

He puts on a gray raincoat and buttons it tightly, pulls a hat with a wide straight brim down over his ears, and, standing before the mirror, puffs out his cheeks and narrows his eyes; he thinks that way he looks even more important than usual. Still puffed up, he goes down in the elevator and walks past the elevator lady, who sits by the telephone with her knitting. She smiles affably at him and says, "Good morning." He forces out a "T'you" through compressed lips, not because he means to treat her badly, but because in his opinion it is improper for him to notice people of such low rank. Near the steps gleams the lacquer and nickel of his personal black Volga; with the appearance of his boss, the chauffeur puts aside his newspaper and turns on the ignition. Sergei Sergeevich plumps down on the seat, carelessly slams the door, and bends his head in that hat slightly, giving the chauffeur the order: Drive! The car dives under the arch and out onto Chernyakhovsky Street, turns onto Krasnoarmeiskaya, rounds the Zhukovsky Academy, and springs out onto Leningrad Prospect. And then it rushes along in the main stream toward the center of the city. The boss sits there, lounging; he narrows his eyes and sometimes widens them, straightens up when one of those officials drives by in his fancy Zil 114 or Chaika, and then screws up his eyes again, full of disdain for everyone else. At the Belorussia Station there's a traffic jam, but not for him—the car crosses the center line and tears along the reserved lane; the traffic cop doesn't even put his whistle to his lips. Of course, it's not a Zil or even a Chaika, but by the color of the car, by the antenna on the roof, by the number on the front bumper, by the hat, the traffic cop's experienced glance can tell that it would be better not to mess with the car's passenger.

Three or four minutes pass and the hat with the straight brim is reflected in the glass door of an exalted institution where the hat's owner holds a high position. The door opens wide and the doorman freezes in a natural half bow.

"Bit of sun today, Sergei Sergeevich," he says politely. Always, when meeting the big bosses, the doorman says something about the current meteorological phenomena.

"Yes, sun," Sergei Sergeevich lets fall offhandedly, without widening his eyes, as if to let him know that the sun is not such a natural marvel but just another of the luminaries personally responsible to him.

Elevator. Corridor. Office. Big desk with telephones. One telephone, which the secretary answers, for everyone, for all those to whom the boss of that office is always either busy or out. With those who sometimes manage to get through on that telephone, Sergei Sergeevich speaks through his teeth, as he does with the doorman or the elevator lady. Another telephone is direct, with no secretary. That is for his wife, his friends and acquaintances. On this telephone the tone is friendly: "Hello, yes, it's me." On the third telephone, the tone is expeditious ("Ivanko here"), and you might even say he was listening attentively. That's the top. Not just anybody calls on that telephone.

The workday begins with approving publication plans. Approving plans is not as easy a matter as it would seem at first glance. You must check the list of writers who plan to publish their books. It is essential to separate the necessary writers from the unnecessary. Necessary writers are the secretaries of the Writers' Union, the directors of publishing houses, the chief editors of journals. You do them a good turn, they do you one: they get you published (if you have something), arrange favorable reviews, consider you a writer, throw some profitable job your way. Necessary writers also include other persons who do not merely write books but who arrange opportunities for side benefits: they find an otter hat or acquire a special pass to a privileged sanatorium or a season ticket to a swimming pool. Unnecessary writers are those who are not able to do any of these things, cannot and do not want to. The most unnecessary ones are Pushkin, Lermontov, Gogol, and other classics—you won't get anything out of them at all. True, sometimes it is necessary to publish them, anyway, but the paper shortage does make itself felt. Yes, that's it, our paper industry is behind, it can't even provide for the necessary writers.

And there sits the owner of that hat, hatless at his desk, working. Necessary writers are underlined, unnecessary ones crossed out.

But (they never let him work) the first visitors have arrived.

Accompanied by a worker from the foreign office of the Writers' Union, Mr. Hopkins enters, tan like all Americans. Doesn't eat bread, doesn't overdo sweets, dilutes his whiskey, is keen on sports: golf, swimming, jogging. Owner of one of the largest publishing houses in the United States. Branches in Canada, the Republic of South Africa, Australia, and New Zealand. "For some passports, a smile on your face; for others, the cold shoulder . . ." If he were a Bulgarian or some other brother in socialism, he could send him on his way. But behind Mr. Hopkins there is international détente and convertible foreign currency. For him, a smile on your face.

"How do you do, Mr. Gopkins, I'm glad to meet you."

"Oh, Mr. Ivanko, do you speak English?"

"Yes, of course, a little."

Mr. Ivanko seats Mr. Hopkins in the place of honor, and over a cup of coffee they talk business like two big publishing specialists. Mr. Hopkins wonders if his colleague Mr. Ivanko couldn't recommend some of the latest novels by the best Russian writers, preferably intellectual prose.

"Hmmm . . . hmmm . . . there's a whole series of intellectual novels about life on the kolkhoz. Won't do? About love? There is one about love. He and she are the characters. He's a good producer—operates several machines simultaneously—but lacks initiative. Works eight stations and is content with that. Naturally, they hassle him about it, and she writes about him on the wall newspaper. That's when they fall in love. The main erotic scene is when she criticizes him at the Komsomol meeting. Of course, he is offended, but later he realizes that she is right and that he loves her. To prove his love to her, he proposes a counterplan—to work twelve stations. A very original plot, colorful language, movements of the machines vividly described. And a happy ending: after a long separation, the heroes meet accidentally at a session of the Supreme Soviet. Only now do they recognize that they cannot live without one another. They stroll down St. George's Hall, through the Palace of Facets, and talk and talk. About counterplans, about raising productivity, about the steady maintenance of labor discipline."

Mr. Hopkins listens with great unfeigned interest. A colossal theme! An unprecedented plot! Unfortunately, he, Mr. Hopkins, doubts that such a book would be successful in the West. The decadent Western reader is used to different kinds of plots. Sex, pornography, rape—

that's what enjoys invariable success in the Western book market.

"We are forced," Mr. Hopkins remarks bitterly, "to follow the readers' tastes."

Mr. Ivanko expresses complete sympathy with his colleague. In that case he cannot offer him anything suitable. Unless, perhaps, the memoirs of Dr. Goebbels.

Oh, Dr. Goebbels! Hopkins's eyes light up. That's exactly what he needs. He's immediately ready to lay out a million dollars, on each of which is a spot of dirt. Well, so what, our country needs it, needs this dirty but hard foreign currency.

After showing Mr. Hopkins out, our respected colleague returns to approving plans, but his secretary comes in and announces Chukovsky's granddaughter.* To hell with her! Couldn't his secretary have told her that he was at a meeting? No, impossible. It seems she found out from someone that he was in his office. Well, all right, all right, show her in. He has to let the air out of his cheeks again and play at being charming. The visitor enters. Oh, he's very glad to see her. Unfortunately, work, work, work, he can't always find the time. What about *Chukokkala*? Of course it must be published. Certainly. And personally he is entirely for it. He is exerting every effort, is occupied with this alone. He is a great admirer of the deceased classic writer. Since childhood he's remembered "The bears rode bikes . . ." Yes, Kornei Ivanovich had a great talent. His death was a huge and irreplaceable loss for children and adults. Yes, absolutely, his literary heritage has great value and we will certainly publish everything worthwhile. But in this case there has been an unexpected

* Kornei Chukovsky: writer, critic, translator; best known for his children's poems, which made his name a byword in nearly every Russian home. See Appendix.

and unpleasant accident. There's been . . . (what can he make up?) . . . an unforeseen event. They were setting the book in the press room, and . . . (hurrah, that's it!) . . . the ceiling collapsed. Just imagine! See how our celebrated builders work. The ceiling collapsed and all the type molds were smashed to smithereens. Of course, the book can be reset, but you understand, we have a planned economy, to set up *Chukokkala* again would mean holding up the whole production line. Naturally, we will get back to this, we'll find a way, but it all takes time. Excuse me, it's the phone. Ivanko speaking, yes, Boris Ivanovich, yes, good, I'll be right there. Once again they won't let us talk, the boss wants me. Call me . . . I'll just take a look, what do we have on our calendar . . . No, this week it's just impossible. Next week . . . hmm . . . hmm . . . Yes, the next is packed full, too . . . So, maybe in two weeks . . . This has been very nice! Very nice!

After showing his guest out, our respected colleague moves on to Boris Ivanovich's office. He enters without ceremony, with a slightly unsteady gait, but with his face and his entire figure expressing great, almost unbearable pleasure at the opportunity of once again beholding Boris Ivanovich with his own eyes.

"Bit of sun today, Boris Ivanovich," he says, as if rejoicing in this perhaps fortuitous, but significant, coincidence.

"Yes, sun," remarks Boris Ivanovich sullenly.

What's with him? Just in a bad mood, or has something happened? Boris Ivanovich is usually friendly, but now . . . Our respected colleague looks at the minister a bit suspiciously.

"Well, now, Sergei Sergeevich." Boris Ivanovich turns his eyes aside. It is terribly unpleasant for him to start this conversation, but what can you do; he raises his head and asks point-blank, "What's going on with that apartment of yours?"

So that's it! Of course, Sergei Sergeevich immediately grasps what the problem is. Someone must have complained. Tattletales! You barely have time to really put the pressure on them before they run off to complain. What people, what pettifoggers!

"You're asking what's with my apartment?" Sergei Sergeevich stalls for time, trying to figure out exactly what Boris Ivanovich knows.

"Yes, I'm asking what's with your apartment."

"Well, after you wrote that letter, Vladimir Fedorovich Promyslov came to a favorable resolution of it, and now the matter is going to be reconsidered at a general assembly of the cooperative."

"You mean, it had already been considered once at a general assembly? Speak up! I'm asking you if the question of improvement of your housing conditions had already been considered at a general assembly?"

"Yes," Sergei Sergeevich forces out.

"Why didn't you make me aware of this?"

"The thing is that I . . . we . . . would have . . . The thing is that the assembly was incompetent." Sergei Sergeevich is at a loss.

"What do you mean, incompetent?"

"It was incompetent because it wasn't the members of the cooperative who were present but their relatives, and besides, they were under pressure."

"Ri-di-cu-lous!" says the minister distinctly.

"What, sir?" Ivanko is himself surprised at his anachronistic formality.

"Never mind the sir," the minister replies sarcastically. "Voinovich has no way of exerting pressure other than presenting his obviously just demands. But you, as I have just found out, really put the pressure on, you've been engaged in extortion and blackmail. See here, my respected colleague, the Party entrusts you with a high post, pays you a large salary, feeds you high-quality food from the distributors, in the hope that you will devote all your energies and time to our literature. But you decided to use your official position and my favorable inclination toward you for personal profit. How can you look people in the eye! And you insist at every turn that you are a Communist. What kind of Communist are you if you abuse your power? By the way, show me the publication plans you've prepared. Well, well, very interesting how your notions of official responsibility are reflected in your plans. So, that's how it is. Why did you include Turganov here? Who needs his undistinguished verses? If you like them so much, publish him in an edition of two—one for him, one for you—but at your own expense. Well, what else? Bulgakov? Is this *the* Bulgakov? Mikhail Afanasievich?* You put him down for an edition of thirty thousand? What? Not enough paper? But there's enough paper for the complete works of Sofronov?† Ah! now I understand why Sofronov entrusted you especially with the editorship of Dreiser's collected works in the Ogonyok Library Edition. And who are these guys, Paderin, Pantielev? There's enough paper for editions of one hundred thousand for them. Have you ever seen anyone looking for a book by Pantielev in the store? Kindly note down Bulgakov for an edition corresponding to the demand. How large? Put down a million copies to start

* Brilliant satirist whose masterpiece, the novel *The Master and Margarita,* was long unpublished in the Soviet Union.

† Anatoly Sofronov: poet, playwright, essayist, member of literary establishment.

with. Why hasn't *Doctor Zhivago* been published yet? What, what? Not written from the correct point of view? Well, have you read even one interesting book written from the correct point of view? Put down a million for *Doctor Zhivago*. You are hereby informed that from now on every worker in this institution will answer for delays of talented works just as people do for delays of freight cars. You say there are hundreds of outrages here and you do not fight against them. It's completely useless. I, my respected colleague, do not need workers like that. I understand, you have a family, you must feed them. I would prefer that you were paid your salary for not working than for work like this. So that's it, my respected colleague, good luck."

Our respected colleague leaves Boris Ivanovich's office, seeing everything as through a fog. Beside himself, he reaches the glass doors. The doorman does not stand up or open the door, and he doesn't mention the weather. Nothing to be surprised at: doormen, janitors, elevator ladies, and chauffeurs are the most knowledgeable public. Somebody says something somewhere and they immediately know everything, and immediately react. Our respected colleague pulls on the door handle—it doesn't give. He pulls harder—no effect. What the devil! Maybe they've already covered all the exits and are about to arrest him for bribery. He pulls the handle with both hands. Easy, no hysterics. You must get control of yourself. There's something written here. Damn it! it says PUSH. It turns out he's never opened this door himself. It was always opened for him and he got used to its opening and closing by itself. Ooof! He's actually sweating. He goes out into the street—it's dark, no sun at all. Like a total eclipse. But in the gathering gloom certain objects and people stand out. There in his personal car sits some efficient character, a boss. They haven't had time to appoint him, but he's already hurrying off somewhere. Where? To publish Bulgakov or Pasternak in an edition of one million? Yes, but how is *he* to get home? On the streetcar? Like everyone else? But he's not used to it. Just a minute ago he was still an important person. Comrade Fedorenko himself was his personal friend . . . But who's that? Riding next to the chauffeur in his private car is Chairman Turganov. Hey, stop, it's me, Sergei Sergeevich, your respected . . . He got wind of it, the old rogue. The rogue gives him an indifferent look and immediately turns away. But coming toward him, waddling just like a duck, is Vera Ivanovna, carrying her body smoothly, majestically. Glad to see you, Vera Ivanovna. You don't recognize me, it's me, your respec . . . Simply Sergei Sergeevich, Seryozha. Remember, I studied with your husband? The Sinologist Ivanko. "You're a Sinologist? My husband always said that one could sooner call a saucepan a Sinologist." Yes . . . Well . . . They've all abandoned me. All turned away. Just this morning they adored me, showered me with smiles, hung on my every word . . . People, people . . .

Enough. We've been fantasizing. Nothing like this happened in real life, of course. Actually, everything was simpler. Boris Ivanovich sent for Sergei Sergeevich on some matter and they discussed that matter first, and then, as if the two things were connected, Boris Ivanovich added, "Oh, Sergei Sergeevich, I completely forgot to tell you: I've heard some slander about you around here from that competitor of yours, damn him. You know, somehow all this isn't turning out too well. No, it's not that, I sympathize with you completely and would be happy to help. I can understand, you've equipped your apartment, there's an opportunity to add on a room, but still you did something that was not quite right. You see what he's driving at—abuse of your official position. There, I'm afraid, I just cannot support you. Neither as director of the committee nor as a Communist. Of course, I don't want to draw any conclusions, but let's put an end to this affair and hit the brakes. I think that you conducted this affair improperly from the very beginning. Went out on a limb, used threats. Why act that way? You're a man of experience, almost a diplomat . . . No, my friend, that's not the way affairs are arranged. I'd be happy to help, but . . ."

Boris Ivanovich threw up his hands . . . and we once again ask the reader's pardon: we made up this monologue, too. Apparently, nothing of the kind happened, at least not right after the minister received our letter. And we know for certain that the minister did receive the letter. And the copies also reached their addressees. And then what? Then nothing. The author of the letter received no answer from his addressees, and since our story doesn't end here, the author assumes that these important persons approved Ivanko's actions.

So!

When a very old official who was in the Soviet government in Lenin's time heard this story, he said, "In my time, there was no worse accusation against a Communist than taking advantage of an official position for personal gain. However," he added, thinking of his twenty-five years in the camps, "our times weren't so perfect either."

Who Is Acting Provocatively?

And still another personage, another important figure comes into our story: Chairman of the Frunzensky Regional Executive Committee, Comrade D. D. Bogomolov. I never saw him personally. Never had the pleasure. But here's how I imagine him. He sits there at a big desk and marks on the papers presented to him: "De-nied!!! You want to exchange something smaller for something bigger. De-nied!!! You want to exchange something bigger for something smaller. De-nied!!! You want to join a co-operative, build a garage, plant a tree in the courtyard. De-nied! De-nied! De-nied!"

Denied . . . When you deny something your power is much more conspicuous than when you approve it. Imagine you're a policeman standing in the street and the cars drive past you. They zip along at modern speeds, the drivers look, barely notice you, if at all. But suppose you blow your whistle, stop a driver and shake him up a bit. Where's he going and what for, why in a car at all and not by streetcar, and where'd he get the money to buy it, and isn't he planning to sell it at a speculative price? Stop and interrogate a second, a third, a fifth, a tenth driver this way: think how many people will notice you then, remember you; in their minds you're almost famous. The same with D. D. Bogomolov. If he'd decided my request immediately and fairly, I, an ingrate, would perhaps not even have remembered his name. But D. D. Bogomolov made an effort and I remember him clearly. After reading my letter to Stukalin, Bogomolov remarked to the man who brought the letter, "See here, Voinovich is acting provocatively. He dictates to whom? A minister. Tells him when he must answer him."

He did not try to decide to whom apartment 66 should belong, he tried to decide who can dictate to whom. By the way, in our humble view, the provocative person is not the one who reminds even a minister of the edicts of the supreme powers but the one who does not comply with these edicts, that is, in this case, the minister himself.

What a Scoundrel!

I'm afraid I'll be accused of slander. Did I really not meet a single positive official on my path? I did. Two. One at first also reprimanded me for acting provocatively, but then said anyway (and thanks to him for this), "Ivanko is acting illegally, but he is powerful. You'll never get in to see Promyslov, but Ivanko can go to see him any time. You can't even imagine what kind of people plead for Ivanko over this telephone." And he stroked the phone with his palm.

The second positive official was a worker at the Central Committee of the CPSU, to whom I managed to tell this story.

"Ivanko?" he asked. "Sergei Sergeevich?"

"Ivanko," I affirmed. "Sergei Sergeevich."

"What a scoundrel!" said my interlocutor, shaking his head.

That was all the reaction I got from the two positive comrades.

What People?

One could guess what kind of people had been pleading over his telephone by Ilin's changed attitude. When I went to him the second time, he was clearly embarrassed, or was pretending to be embarrassed. No, I think he really was embarrassed.

"You count on me to call Promyslov up. But what will

I say to him? The cooperative is an autonomous organization, it is not subordinate to the Writers' Union. Do something yourself. What am I to tell you? All the pensioners know where to turn in situations like this. And you, a writer, a satirist, can't figure it out. Go to the First Secretary of the Regional Committee."

"I'm non-Party."

"What's the difference? Ivanko's a Party member."

"But this secretary won't see me."

"Well, you just make sure he does."

Well, all right, suppose he does. If this weren't a documented history taken straight from life, if it were a novel, written according to the tenets of socialist realism, then there really would be a happy ending in the Regional Committee Office. In how many of our novels does an appeal to the Regional Committee end all the anxieties of the literary heroes. In the Regional Committee, evil suffers defeat, while justice triumphs.

When I got home from Ilin's, I called the Frunzensky Regional Executive Committee to find out the name of the first secretary. They told me: "Pirogov, Evgeny Andreevich."

I remembered: the Planet Press, the Torch Press, and some Pirogov from the City Committee.

That's it. The circle is complete. To the legion supporters of Ivanko we are obliged to add yet another rather important figure. Well, now it's time to come to some conclusions, time to arrange in order of importance the public servants who, over such a trivial matter, headed toward direct violation of Soviet law itself. Here they are, these public servants: Board Chairman of the Moscow Writers' Housing Cooperative, Chairman of the Review Committee of the HC, Chairman of the Regional Executive Committee, First Secretary of the Regional Committee, Secretary (actually Director) of the Writers' Union of the U.S.S.R., Chairman of the State Committee, the Deputy Chairman, Party Organization Secretary of the Committee, and Chairman of the Moscow Soviet. All these people (and two of them members of the Central Committee of the CPSU) direct our lives from top to bottom; they are the very ones who embody, at least within the limits of Moscow, what we usually call *the Soviet regime.*

"Aha!" says the vigilant reader. "That's what he's getting at! So this story is anti-Soviet."

Yes. Perhaps. But, citizen judges, please note that it was not I who created this story but those very people I have listed here. I did everything in my power to keep it from happening this way.

Curiosity Is No Crime

Well then, what was I to do, anyway?

My supporters said, "Watch it, they'll get you to do something illegal. Don't yield to provocation. Act exclusively within the limits of the law."

Of course, this is one view: to resist the illegal acts of the authorities with one's own legal acts. Later on, when I'm still in my single room and have to work there and listen to the baby cry, I'll be able to take comfort in the fact that I didn't go beyond the limits of the law. And Ivanko, after he expands his space for his new toilet, will experience pangs of conscience at not having acted legally.

Under pressure from my supporters, I wrote a letter to yet another of the insignificant boards they suggested. This time I wrote unprovocatively. I wrote as they asked me to—mentioned my proletarian past, listed literary accomplishments, and, stressing my wife's pregnancy, humbly begged that they give my request their attention.

I did not receive an answer from this board either, but then I didn't expect one. I had lost faith in the effectiveness of legal action. I conceived other plans, which my supporters warned me against and whose implementation was eagerly awaited in my opponents' camp.

"Just let him make one unauthorized move," said Vera Ivanovna, "and then he'll see what'll happen to him."

She did not know that our interests had already begun to converge. I myself was also curious to see what would happen to me.

I decided to satisfy Vera Ivanovna's desire and . . .

The Unauthorized Move

. . . As Chairman Turganov subsequently informed the members of the board, on April 26, 1973, a most deplorable event occurred in the cooperative. An extraordinary incident took place which went beyond the tolerable limits of our moral code. To be exact, on the morning of the day mentioned, two persons were seen dragging out of entranceway 7 an object resembling a sofa-bed. The object was then dragged into entranceway 4. This movement of persons and chattel was immediately reported to the Chairman. And when two persons with the abovementioned object burst into entranceway 4, the elevator lady was already justifying herself on the telephone.

"Yes, they're moving in! What am I supposed to do? I can't hold them back! I'm a woman, they won't listen to me."

Shortly afterward, the object resembling a sofa-bed (which turned out to be precisely that) found itself in apartment 66. After the sofa, there followed in quick succession a refrigerator, a typewriter, a television set, four chairs, and the building manager. The last was slightly drunk, but still on his feet. From his words, one could make out (not without some difficulty) that the building manager was expressing displeasure at the incident and offering his services for returning the chattels to their point of origin.

"What are you doing?" said the building manager. "How can you, you have to ask me for this, and you go ahead and . . ."

With these words he seized the sofa-bed and attempted to move it toward the door. However, on receiving a hundred and twenty rubles from the man in charge of the moving, he decided not to exert himself.

"Understand," he said, brushing off his hands, "I don't need this. I've been in the Party since '32. I'm a colonel."

"What branch?" I asked, curious, looking him in the eye.

He winced and said hastily, "I'm a political worker."

"A political worker in which branch?"

"I'm a political worker," he repeated uncertainly and backed toward the door. "I have medals down to there!" he added and went out to the stairs.

You, of course, have guessed in which branch he served and for what actions he received his medals. An honorable service, of course, but still it's awkward.

Nocturnal Terrors

Night. I am alone in my empty apartment. I lie on the folding bed and, like my hero Chonkin (they say writers repeat the fates of their heroes), await attack from every quarter. What forces will the powerful Ivanko pit against me? Will they break down the door or make a landing on the balcony? It's late. I want to go to sleep. But I shouldn't sleep. My eyelids are drooping. Dead silence beyond the wall that separates me from Ivanko's apartment. Are they asleep? Maybe they're breaking through over there? "Don't sleep," I say to myself. "Don't sleep . . ." Suddenly the wall cracks and collapses before my eyes. It collapses noiselessly, just like a silent movie. Whole pieces of brickwork fall out, a cloud of dust rises, and everything is obscured. But then the dust settles and—what's this I see? Into the room, through the breach in the wall, astride an improbably blue, diamond-studded toilet, rides our respected colleague. Triumphantly, he waves some authorization, a Party card, a Writers' Union membership card, an official identity card, a travel identity card, and a letter with Stukalin's signature certifying that the bearer is an important person. Clanking its caterpillar treads, the toilet descends on me.

"I'll crush you-ou-ou-ou!" the toilet driver intones.

I open my eyes and gradually come to. The wall is intact. Everything is quiet. Outside the open vent window, the wind is howling—*ou-ou-ou!* . . .

Ilin Again

"So, Viktor Nikolaevich," I said, "I've come to you for the last time."

He grinned. "You aren't giving up?"

"I'm giving up. I see that it's useless to come to you. You promised to stand up for me, and now you wash your hands of it. When you had to work me over for signing letters or for *Chonkin*, there were a lot of you here. The committees were working, the secretariat met.

Now you have a clear criminal case before you. Two members of your organization, abusing their positions, attempt to slip each other bribes, and where's the secretariat? Where are the committees? Why don't you cry for help?"

Ilin turned his eyes away. "Yes, but I've heard that you've been unwilling to compromise, too."

"You mean I'm being difficult?"

He pondered, realizing that this formula was not new to me. "I don't say that you're being difficult, but apparently they've offered you some alternatives and you won't agree to them."

"And I will not agree to them."

"Why not?"

"How can I explain it to you . . ."

"On principle?" he suggested.

"Oh, so you do know that word."

"So what do you want from me?"

"I want you to act on principle, too, but if you can't, then forget it. I came to tell you, if you don't know already, that I moved into that apartment."

"How?"

"The usual way. Dragged the things in, took out the old locks, put in new ones. Here are the keys." As a visual aid, I rattled the keys under his nose.

"It was a mistake for you to do that," he said. "Before, you were acting legally, but now you're laying yourself open. I told you and I tell you again: go see the Secretary of the Regional Committee. You'll be evicted."

"That's exactly what I wanted to talk to you about. I hope that you won't keep our conversation a secret, but that you'll tell Ivanko's patrons that I will not move out of that apartment under any sort of pressure. Except maybe if they carry me and my pregnant wife out in their arms. That should be a very interesting spectacle, and I can promise you there will be spectators. And if this story has already gone beyond the boundaries of the cooperative, I'm not so sure it won't go beyond other boundaries as well."

The general's eyes looked shifty behind his glasses. He was considering what to say, while I watched him curiously. I was waiting for him to ask, "What are you suggesting?"

"Just tell that to the Secretary of the Regional Committee," he said, much to my surprise.

When I got home, I received a summons. I was ordered to appear before Assistant Regional Public Prosecutor of Civil Proceedings Comrade L. N. Yakovleva on April 28 at 10 a.m.

At the Prosecutor's Office

April 28, 1973. 10 a.m. Small room. In the corner, a five-liter can of cucumbers. A large woman is sitting at the desk. Without interrupting her telephone conversation, she motions toward a chair by the window. I sit down. I unintentionally listen in. She's arranging with someone for the coming holiday. The conversation is particularly businesslike. Easter is almost on top of us, guests on the first, and nothing is ready yet, at Eliseevsky's emporium on Gorky Street they've put out sturgeon and cod liver . . . What? A cake? What cake? You'd have to get in line for it first thing in the morning . . . Someone with nothing to do can do that . . . Well, yes, your husband . . . How can you survive now on just one salary? . . .

I sit, I listen, I think of my own problems. Of course, Such People have already phoned her. They've already told her everything. Now we'll start the riddle of the chicken or the egg. She will ask why I made an unauthorized move. I will say that it was not unauthorized, that there is the decision of the assembly, here I have a copy of the minutes. The copy, of course, does not interest her, she's interested in the authorization. No authorization—move out. What's it to her? She has the holiday . . . She's thinking about how she can get her hands on something . . . And here . . . And naturally, you won't prove anything . . . What a disgusting woman . . . They're all the same, they're all made of the same cloth. I'll tell her: You are the Public Prosecutor, you should see to the observance of the law, and you . . .

"Well, then." Putting down the phone, she looks at me with a smile that portends no good. "So, you moved into someone else's apartment without authorization."

"How can I explain?" I mumble, knowing in advance that all explanations are superfluous. "Not exactly someone else's and not exactly without authorization."

Smiling ironically, she nods her head. Naturally, she didn't expect to hear anything different. There has never been a single unauthorized squatter who has not tried to prove that he is innocent.

"Well, tell me how it happened."

I tell her and see by her eyes that she's bored. She has her own troubles. She has to make a practical decision. If they're to evict, then it must be today. Tomorrow the holidays begin, the police won't have time to mess around, and she won't find any witnesses. Most likely, he especially counted on it's being the eve of a holiday. The holiday is four days. For four days he'll be living in someone else's apartment, for four days he'll be breaking the law. No, that cannot be tolerated, urgent measures must be taken, because in the food store across the street they're giving out fillet of bureaucrat . . . Pah! Damn, he's driving me crazy! She raises unseeing eyes. "What bureaucrat?"

"At our cooperative," I repeat hastily, "a certain bureaucrat has set up house."

"What's this bureaucrat got to do with it? I'm not interested in him."

I'll say!

"If you want to know the circumstances, you must know about the bureaucrat. The thing is that he occupies an important post on the state publishing committee and, using his position . . ."

"I tell you, I am not at all interested in the bureaucrat. I'm asking you if you have moved into apartment 66."

"I have."

"Well, then."

"But not without authorization."

"But it says here, it was without authorization."

"But does it say there that the general assembly gave me this apartment?"

"Hmm . . ." she looks through the letter again. "No, it doesn't."

"In that case, I ask you to familiarize yourself with this document."

I hand her the paper. The Assistant Public Prosecutor reads. Excerpt from the minutes of the general assembly. (Don't ask me how I tricked the building manager out of it.) Discussed, resolved, to grant Voinovich . . . A round seal . . .

"Ye-e-s . . . This does change things. One moment." She moves the telephone toward her, dials a number. "Sergei Dmitrievich, we've got a letter here from the Moscow Writers' Cooperative about an illegal move. You know about it? But the comrade submitted an excerpt from the minutes of the assembly. What? There was no quorum? Then get a quorum together; but until then I cannot approve the eviction. What? The letter from Comrade Promyslov? I understand, but with all due respect to Comrade Promyslov, under no circumstances will I be an accessory to a violation of the law. That's all, the matter is finished. Happy holidays. Thank you." She puts down the phone, turns to me. "Well then, you heard it all. For now, I do not have grounds for your eviction. So—forge ahead. Good luck!"

The murk disperses. At last I have found an official who has not forgotten that laws exist. What a nice woman, what a charming woman! And how soundly she rebuked that Budarin: "That's all, the matter is finished." And that was that! She would not be an accessory to a violation of the law. With all due respect to Comrade Promyslov.

The Impeachment Process

We have reached the point where the plot of our absorbing narrative forks. However, neither branch strays very far from the other, they run parallel and intertwine. The first branch is a continuation of our struggle for apartment 66 (it is by no means over). The second is devoted to a description of the process of Chairman Turganov's dismissal from power, a process which, as we now know, is called impeachment. Once again the Watergate affair comes to mind.

Who among us, following its peripeteia on the foreign radio broadcasts, was not amazed? My heavens, what was all the commotion about? The President of the greatest country on earth wanted to eavesdrop on someone. That's all there was to it. We, who grew up under different conditions, couldn't even understand clearly the nature of the problem. We didn't even know that a chief of state should be removed from his post for such nonsense. If you don't want to be overheard, cover the telephone with a pillow, turn on the radio, go to the bathroom and converse in a whisper over the noise of the toilet flushing at the same time, or even better, use paper and pencil for communication, burn the evidence, grind the ashes into powder and throw them to the winds. But all this confusion over the tapes just makes no sense at all. If the President of the United States had been not Nixon but our Chairman Turganov, he would have rubbed the tapes off the face of the earth, or burned them together with the building where they were stored. Yet, even in his position, Turganov demonstrated no little inventiveness in the area of petty intrigues.

But before getting down to a description of the impeachment process on the small scale of our building, I should analyze the balance of power on the board and how it changed in the course of our plot's development. During the period described, the board was composed of eleven persons. The twelfth was Chairman of the Review Committee Bunina, who took a most active part in the affair.

Of the twelve, four actively supported Ivanko's side from the very beginning: Ivanko himself, Turganov, Bunina, and a certain Kuleshov, a sportswriter and, incidentally, as they say, the son of Alexander Blok and Baroness Nolle. This magnificent foursome was ready to do anything to accomplish its goal. The fifth member of the board was on leave, the sixth was vacillating, wishing to seem like an honest man and at the same time wishing not to spoil his relations with the powerful Ivanko. In private conversations with the tenants of our building, he assured them that his sympathies lay with

Voinovich, but on the board he raised his hand for Ivanko. The seventh member would always run over to the side that seemed strongest to him at a given moment, pretending that he was an ignorant man of the East, and a bit of a poet to boot, not of this world and not too clear about what was going on. The eighth, an academician and Hero of Labor, decided that for him to participate in this squabble was not at all becoming, so he maintained complete neutrality and did not appear at the board meetings, despite impassioned appeals from both sides. Thus, at the beginning of our story, there were six persons on Ivanko's side, including the two vacillators, and on mine—four. Two of the four considered my demands just and respected my literary activities, the other two paid no attention to the second factor, deciding only on the basis of the legal side of the matter. One must take into account that even these four had to consider Ivanko's threats to some extent; they were all writers, they all wanted to publish, and for that reason they acted (and I am grateful to them for this) according to principle, but with circumspection.

Besides the quantitative advantage on Ivanko's side, there was a qualitative one. Turganov was not simply one of our respected colleague's six followers but the Chairman of the board. It was he who called the board meetings. He tried to select a time when one of my supporters was absent. During Ivanko's absence, he did not convene the board at all, using various pretexts: he was tired, he had no time, he was sick. And there was yet another factor on their side: their energy and purposefulness. Of my supporters, one was a hockey fan and skipped board meetings if the Czech-Soviet game was being shown at the same time, another had a pool pass and went swimming. Ivanko's minions, when necessary, did not watch hockey, did not go to the pool, appeared at the board, and fought together for the interests of their protégé. But gradually my supporters started to stir, too. They began to notice that they were being deceived and led by the nose. They could not but be affected by public opinion among the tenants of our building, opinion which was gradually becoming more and more heated. Finally, another member of the board returned after a long absence, an energetic man and one independent of Ivanko. What angered him most of all was Ivanko's intention to demolish a main wall, which he believed would deform the entire building. He immediately declared that under no circumstances would he endure the destruction of the building. The situation began to change. Sensing a strong hand, my supporters united beneath the banner of the returnee. And, when he saw that the balance of power had begun to change, the member who wished to seem honest quit the game and stopped appearing at the meetings altogether. The man-of-the-East-and-poet, after some vacillation, ran over to the opposing camp. Bunina, too, was caught in the cross fire. "I'm for Voinovich," she proclaimed, "but the truth is, he just wants a good apartment." However, we've heard that from her before.

A Bit More about Turganov

When Turganov's position had already become quite unstable, he announced at one of the board meetings that he could not be dismissed from office without the approval of the appropriate Party organs. Just a month before, this argument might have been persuasive. Now it was perceived merely as a demagogic ruse. In answer to his announcement, Turganov was told that he had been elected chairman without such approval and for that reason could be removed without it, too. "And besides," someone asked, "why should we consult the Party organs if you are non-Party?"

Frankly, the news that Turganov was non-Party surprised me. That such a person had not attached himself to the ruling party seemed completely incredible to me. If he did not do so, it meant there were serious reasons. Either he had been in the Party and had been expelled, or he had never had the opportunity to join it. Why not? He did not have, and could not have had, of course, any moral objections to joining the Party. That meant there were some black spots on his record that even the Party considered black. Knowing that he was from Kiev, I admit, much as I regret it, that I thought maybe he'd been in the Polizei under the Germans. The impression this man gave allowed me to think that he was ready to express his devotion to any regime that seemed to him sufficiently stable. And in Kiev, under the Germans, the regime seemed stable to many people. And, of course, I would not have been surprised to learn that Turganov turned Jews and Communists over to the Germans, since he belonged to neither group.

But knowledgeable people told me that Turganov had not been in Kiev under the Germans. He had been there before the war, and actively collaborated with the NKVD, landing eighteen persons in prison, his colleagues. Later he did something else for which he almost landed in prison himself; he quickly moved to Moscow, and then the war started and the Kiev branch couldn't get at Turganov. Consequently, I was mistaken about Turganov's career in the Polizei, but not much. A person who destroys his colleagues for his personal well-being is a scoundrel. And it matters not at all whether he does it with the help of the Gestapo or resorts to the services of his own country's organs.

An Interesting Proposition

As I said above, of course, I wanted to stay in the apartment, but any other outcome of the affair suited me, too. I was willing to experiment to see how far the power of my rival extended, to reach certain general conclusions to the question: Have we come to a state of complete lawlessness or do some limits still exist?

Naturally, only one outcome suited my rival—victory. Now he needed it not only for the gratification of his territorial desires but for his prestige. "If he doesn't get his way, they might fire him from his job," one of my friends said. "This is their ethic: If you can't finish it, don't start it."

And so the author of these lines received new propositions. Turganov passed on through a third person, "So ask Voinovich why he's acting this way. After all, we still have to live, and in one building. He'll have a child soon, and two rooms won't be enough for him. And by the way, there'll be a three-room apartment opening up soon, and I promise it will be his; I'm ready to give any sort of promissory note . . ."

So that's what it came to, they were ready to give a promissory note. A false promissory note, of course.

But that's not all. Some time later, May 3 to be precise, a famous writer, satirist, and humorist appeared at the new apartment of the writer of these lines. He came to inquire how we were settled in the new place. He looked over the walls, ceilings, kitchen. He approved.

"Not a bad apartment. It was worth fighting a bit for an apartment like this. But incidentally, I've brought you some very interesting information. I was at the newspaper on business and suddenly I heard this bit of news: they say there are three rent-free two-room apartments at the Writers' Union and one of them is reserved for . . . For whom, do you think? For you. An excellent apartment. Forty square meters . . . How many do you have here? Thirty-five? That means another five meters, plus a whole lot of extras, a storeroom, a hall, and all that, and, best of all, it's rent-free. The five or six thousand you'd get for your apartment from the cooperative wouldn't be so bad, either."

"Well, of course, five or six thousand is real money for me."

"I'd be sorry to part with a neighbor like you, but I think you should agree to it. By the way, Simonov just returned from Yalta and was very interested in you. I dropped in to see him and he immediately asked how Voinovich was doing. So I told him what I knew. 'You know,' he said, 'Ivanko came to see me and asked me to have a talk with Voinovich. But how am I supposed to talk with Voinovich if I barely know him? He'll send me on my way and rightly so.' 'No,' I said to him, 'of course he won't send you on your way, but what will you say to him? That he should live in one room so that Ivanko can live in four?' 'That, of course, is true,' he said. 'But, you know, Ivanko does an awful lot for us. We just got Bulgakov through because of him. The others wouldn't agree for anything, but he gave the okay.' That's the way the conversation went. But here's what I have to say to you about the apartment: agree. No, don't just give in right away. Say that you have to think it over, see what kind of apartment it is, knock your price up a bit, and then agree. So what do you think? Am I right?"

"How can I explain?" I answered. "You see, I wasn't

fighting for this apartment just because I needed it badly. I told everyone I was struggling for it on principle. And now people will think that Ivanko couldn't frighten me off, so he bought me for money."

My guest was surprised. "Well, my friend, that's ridiculous. To hell with all your considerations, take the money and move."

"Well, of course I would move, that's the point. But only if I were given a guarantee that Ivanko wouldn't get this apartment."

Only later did I figure out that my guest had come on instructions. How could I not have known right away? I was to pretend that I was wavering and wait for the official offer. True, it would have complicated our already rather involved plot.

Several days later I learned that the apartment under discussion was given to the writer Pilyar.

Lucky him!

The Progressive Sergei Sergeevich

Have you noticed a certain change in our respected colleague's tactics? If before he acted only from a position of power, rattling his saber and his connections, he now sent his rival positive reports of himself through his intermediaries. You see, he's a progressive, they got Bulgakov through because of him. How could I not let him have the apartment after that? Really, it would have been very unpleasant for me to have been the reason for Bulgakov's not being published.

(Some time after the conclusion of this story, a volume of Bulgakov really did come out. An excellent edition in a beautiful binding. *The Master and Margarita*, complete, with no cuts; they even left in the scene about buying foreign goods in the torgsin store. And yet we ingrates do not thank our respected colleague for this edition. We, Bulgakov's readers and admirers, cannot obtain this edition. Of course, I do not have myself in mind. If I'd let our respected colleague have the apartment, I could probably have counted on one copy. The book was not published for us, but for readers abroad, who hardly need it since they have access to publications from the émigré house Possev. Twenty-six thousand of the total printing of thirty thousand went abroad. And in the Writers' Union, they say, fifteen copies were distributed among the members of the Secretariat (for some reason they don't want each other's books, but Bulgakov's, a man they hounded to death). And I have no doubt that Bulgakov stands on our respected colleague's shelf. Not as a favorite writer, but as a sign of prestige not available to just anybody.

And here's another reproach from a progressive position. When Boris Gribanov, a worker at Goslitizdat, met Vladimir Kornilov, he started complaining that he had always respected Voinovich as a writer and an honest man, but now he was grieved and disappointed to learn that Voinovich, it turned out, wrote denunciations.

"Denunciations?" Kornilov was surprised. "To whom and of whom?"

"What do you mean? He's written Stukalin about Ivanko."

"Well, what was there left for him to do?"

Gribanov answered nothing to this, but said that Voinovich still wouldn't get the apartment.

"He'll get it," said Kornilov.

Having bet a bottle of cognac, the two parted.

In the interests of plot, an explanation of the motives guiding Gribanov must be put off to the end of our tale. But right now, I'll say that Gribanov was by no means moralizing idly, either. A year later, with Ivanko's help, he left for the United States as director of the Soviet book exhibition.

From the Chairman's Epistolary Storehouse

Let's look in on the next meeting of the board. There, at the desk, holding his briefcase before him with two hands, stands the Chairman, nodding his egg-shaped head. But why does he have such a hesitant look? Oh, can it be he's trying to justify himself? It turns out he was asked why he wrote a letter to the public prosecutor's office all by himself, without notifying the other members of the board. The question, of course, was rightly asked, perhaps in the present case a small error had been committed, but as Chairman he was obliged to take the most effective measures to avert unauthorized activities. But did the Chairman inform the public prosecutor that the apartment Voinovich moved into had been granted him by the general assembly? No, he did not inform her of this. Why not? Well, you see, comrades, it turns out that the assembly that originally voted Voinovich the apartment was not competent. In our building, there are 132 members of the cooperative. A quorum is 88. But at the assembly there were only 79. Aha, but at the same meeting an apartment was granted to the writer Laskin's daughter, who received her order a whole month ago. So, then, there was a quorum for her but not for Voinovich? Tell you what, old man, the board advises, you will have to withdraw your letter from the prosecutor's office. No, the Chairman answers with dignity, he cannot do that. All right, they tell him, we shall spare your self-esteem, but in that case you will write an addendum to your letter, to the effect that the apartment was granted to Voinovich by the general assembly. The Chairman snorts but agrees. They note in the minutes, "Comrade Turganov obliged to . . ."

Comrade Turganov goes home and fulfills his obligation: "As an addendum to my letter of such-and-such, I beg to inform you that apartment 66 was granted to Voinovich by the general assembly. But," he continues, "as is apparent from the minutes, section 13, this assembly was not competent, in view of the absence of a quorum. In spite of this, Voinovich continues to occupy apartment 66 illegally and, simultaneously, apartment 138. As one who is responsible to the Regional Executive Committee for maintenance of law and order, I demand Voinovich's immediate eviction . . ."

Two days passed and the board again convened. Later on it convened again, and again, and many times more. A resolution was adopted to send a letter to the Regional Executive Committee requesting that this matter be concluded as soon as possible with the issue of an authorization to Voinovich. Did the Chairman agree to the text of the letter? Yes, he agreed and was ready to affix his signature. The letter was retyped and brought for signature, but the Chairman left all the copies at home. What did he do with them? Tear them up? What do you mean, they said, he wouldn't dare. He dared to write to the public prosecutor's office. Everyone gave his opinion. They said, the letter was written on one sheet of paper, and the signatures—since they wouldn't fit—on another. So, couldn't he affix these signatures to a new text? How could he? they said. That would be a clearly criminal act. But up to then, as we have seen, he had not been distinguished for excessive scrupulousness in his choice of means. Still, we suspected the Chairman unjustly. On May 16 it was learned that two letters arrived at the

Regional Executive Committee. One, as we know, above the signatures of all the members of the board except Turganov, and another, of completely contradictory content, above the Chairman's signature.

Grammar and Arithmetic

May 17. Chairman of the Frunzensky Regional Executive Committee Comrade Bogomolov announced that the following Wednesday without fail he would study this question and decide it definitely. That was not true. He had decided it the day before. But not definitely, since it did not depend on him. On May 16, he signed a document containing the following: "Ct. Voinovich, Vladimir Nikolaevich, denied grant of apt. 66, 34.9 sq. m. in size, inasmuch as already provided with living space. His family of 2 persons (he, wife) occupy a one-room apartment, 24.41 sq. m. in size.

"Decision by the general assembly of the Moscow Writers' Housing Cooperative of March 11 of this year disaffirmed, since it is not competent, inasmuch as it was adopted by an insufficient number of votes of the Housing Cooperative members."

Dmitri Dmitrievich:
On familiarizing myself with your letter, I was extremely perplexed. In the first place, what does "Ct." mean? Once, titles of nobility were designated in abbreviated form: "Ct." was count, "Pr." was prince. Several of my ancestors really were counts. In honor of one of them, chief commander of the Black Sea fleet, Admiral Marco Ivanovich Voinovich, a famous pier at Sevastopol today bears the name Count's Landing. Does your "Ct." mean that my noble title has been returned to me? In that case, I

beg you to decide the question of restoration of my family arms, which I shall nail to the doors of apartment 66, as soon as I receive the order for it.

In the second place, it seems to me that you are somewhat at odds with Russian grammar. Otherwise, you would know that the name Voinovich declines in all six cases, just like any other. If you continue not to decline such names, you might be taken for a foreigner.*

In the third place, your knowledge in the field of arithmetic is appalling. Let's do some figuring. Each of the two persons you mention has the right to 9 sq. meters of space. $9 \times 2 = 18$. But you know very well that one of those two persons (I) have the right to 20 sq. meters of additional space as a member of the Writers' Union. $18 + 20 = 38$. Right? And if you figure that the second person (my wife) is in a pregnant state with a third person (which you also know), we must perform yet another computation: $38 + 9 = 47$ sq. meters. If we add to this another 3 sq. meters, which are due a family, we get a round 50. So you see. But you refuse me 35 meters, and not of public but of cooperative space, that is, space acquired at my own expense.

Having read your letter, Dmitri Dmitrievich, I decided that you

a. are insufficiently educated for your post and

b. either do not know our laws or, even worse, consciously violate them.

In any case, you discredit the Soviet regime, which through your office you represent.

I remain, ever, at your service,

Ct. V. Voinovich

* Russian declines only personal and family names that fit neatly into its own grammatical categories. By not declining "Voinovich," the official hints that it is a foreign, i.e., Jewish, name.

Actually, I wrote this letter but did not send it. The matter was coming to an end one way or another, and Bogomolov's refusal was my last attempt to oblige Those People, whom I did not want to give in to at all. I set the letter aside and include it in my work now just to enliven the narrative.

Continuation of the Impeachment Process

May 18. Board meeting, without Turganov this time. Turganov had fallen ill. "Let whoever went to the public prosecutor's office inquire at the polyclinic whether I am really ill," he told the board.

Discussed: Board Chairman B. A. Turganov's irregular conduct.

Resolved: Comrade Turganov required to explain his actions in writing by May 22. Until presentation of the written explanations and their examination, B. A. Turganov to be relieved of his duties as board chairman.

S. S. Ivanko's spoken declaration of resignation from membership on the board considered and his request approved.

How's that for an impeachment process? But it wasn't over yet.

•

May 21. Turganov recovered, came to the office, and took the minutes of the board meeting home.

•

May 21. Ivanko announced that he was not resigning from the board, and that his statement that he did not wish to participate in these squabbles applied only to those specific squabbles. How do you like that?

•

May 21. Kozlovsky announced that he had not resigned

from the Review Committee, either. So we must have misunderstood him at the assembly.

•

May 21. Turganov wrote to the board that he was ready to give an account of his actions, only not by May 22 but "at an appropriate time."

•

May 25. Dyarchy. The new chairman set a board meeting for the next day. Turganov sent round a counterorder to the members of the board: "By order of the Chief [with a capital letter, of course. V.V.] of the Cooperative Department of the Moscow Municipal Housing Administration, Comrade G. M. Chekalina, the board meeting set for May 26 is postponed until agreement with her is reached. The day of the meeting will be announced subsequently."

•

May 25. The board's answer to Turganov: "We wish to remind you that in accord with the bylaws of the Housing Cooperative, the Cooperative Department has the right to approve a decision of the board or the general assembly but may not determine the time of board meetings . . ."

•

May 25. A historic conversation. One of the board members called our respected colleague Sergei Sergeevich and informed him that, inasmuch as he had not resigned from membership on the board, he was invited to tomorrow's meeting. The question of Turganov's removal from the office of chairman would be decided. He would not be able to come? He was busy? What a pity! In that case, one would like to know his point of view. Sergei Sergeevich readily informed him that he had no objections to Turganov's removal. Since the Chairman abused his power and the confidence of the collective, he, Sergei

Sergeevich Ivanko, as a Communist, must resolutely censure him.

Several days later, a new piece of news reached us: at a meeting of some high board, Ivanko completely wrecked the chances of the Turganov collection (in two volumes?) that was being prepared for publication.

What can you say? You know who your friends are when times are bad.

•

May 26. Discussed and resolved: B. A. Turganov dismissed. But do you think things ended there? Certainly not.

•

May 27. Turganov's letter to the board: "Inasmuch as, despite the agreement with the Chief of the Cooperative Department of the Moscow Municipal Housing Administration, Comrade G. M. Chekalina, concerning postponement of the board meeting, such was, in any case, conducted in the absence of a representative of the Moscow Municipal Housing Administration, I am obliged to bring this to the attention of the *Regulative Organs* [italics mine. V.V.] and, until receipt of orders, have no right to begin surrender of board duties."

Things were coming to a head. On one of the days I've described, the telephone rang in my new apartment.

"This is Bakharov from the Regional Executive Committee speaking. Why haven't you obeyed our order? Why have you not vacated the apartment you have moved into without authorization?"

"Who are you, anyway?" I asked.

"I told you who I am. Vacate the apartment immediately, you vile pig."

I immediately regarded this call as Shabashkin did Dubrovsky's letter, that is, the call produced a favorable impression on me. I understood that things were bad for my opponents.

Soon the *Regulative Organs* capitulated.

"Convene an assembly with a quorum," they informed us. "It will be as it decides."

End of the Impeachment Process

TO ALL MEMBERS OF THE MOSCOW WRITERS' HOUSING COOPERATIVE

Dear Comrades:

The board of the cooperative considers it its duty to inform you that a sharp dispute has arisen among the cooperative leadership, making management of the building not only difficult but impossible. There is no way out of this extraordinary and unprecedented situation except by calling a general assembly. A quorum is essential if the assembly is to have full power. That is why we urgently request each member of the cooperative to attend the general assembly on Thursday, May 31, at 8 p.m. at the Polyclinic. We earnestly entreat you to consider the seriousness of our position and fulfill your duty in our general interests.

(In the event that your personal attendance is impossible, we ask you to give power of attorney to a member of your family, by which you indicate that you entrust them both to speak and to vote in your place, since otherwise your vote cannot be counted.)

•

May 29 and 30. The women activists made the rounds of the apartments, pleading, "Please keep the evening of the thirty-first free . . . come . . . very necessary, very important. It's vital."

•

May 31. The general assembly. More than enough for a quorum—111 persons. Brief account of Chairman Turganov's activities. Motion: to remove him from board membership. Accepted unanimously. No, one abstention; he doubts such a decision may be taken without hearing Turganov out. Objection: How could we hear someone out if he wasn't there? He's not here, some say, but his letter is. The letter was read. The author of the letter believes that the assembly cannot properly understand his actions. That can be done only by a special commission, which is to be set up in the near future by the Writers' Union and the Regional Executive Committee. Until such time as the commission evaluates his activities, he will continue to consider himself Chairman.

"Well, that's clear," said the abstainer. "I withdraw my abstention."

Turganov was removed. Who was next? Someone mentioned that since Kozlovsky, as he said, had resigned from the Review Committee at the last assembly, why keep him? Especially since . . . They made signs to the speaker, shushed him: we shouldn't touch anyone else, everything should be quiet and smooth, Turganov was removed, now everything's in order. What do you mean? What kind of order is that, when you drive out one swindler and the rest stay? Now I couldn't endure any more and stood up.

"Comrades, what do you mean?" I said. "It isn't just Turganov. Turganov didn't act for himself alone. Since we're all gathered here, why shouldn't we at the same time remove the one who—"

They started winking and making signs to me: quiet,

quiet, everything's in order. Well, I suppose everything really was in order. The main thing had been accomplished: Turganov had been driven out, our respected colleague had not gotten his fourth room and probably never would in this building, and even his membership on the board wouldn't help him. But I wanted to draw him into the light and show the gathering who he was and what he represented.

Quiet! Quiet! Sh-h-h!

The second question was put to a vote: Grant V. N. Voinovich apartment 66. It was as if there never had been any other candidates. We voted: 110 for, 1 abstention. Everything proceeded quietly. After the assembly, someone joked that before we dispersed we should convene a new assembly to confirm the decision of this assembly, which had confirmed the decision of the previous assembly, which had confirmed the decision of the assembly previous to it.

•

On a sunny day in the middle of July, I met our building manager in the courtyard. He came up to me and extended his hand as an equal to an equal. I thought he was about to inform me of his military rank and Party service record and present his pension book. For that reason, after allowing him to shake my hand a bit, I immediately pulled it out of his, intending to vanish under the entrance gate; however, the building manager's words surprised me so much that I stood as if rooted to the ground.

"Listen," said the building manager. "Why don't you take the passports down for registration?"*

* Soviet citizens over the age of sixteen are obliged to possess a passport. Changes in place of residence, employment, and marital status are entered on passports for the purpose of supervision and regulation.

"What?" I said distrustfully. "The passports?"

"Well, yes, the passports. Yours and your wife's."

"You mean, for registration?" I asked, looking searchingly into the building manager's eyes and wondering if there weren't some trap behind all this. You bring the passports and sometimes instead of the PERMANENTLY REGISTERED stamp, they print DISCHARGED. (By the way, that had already happened to me once. At the Communal Housing Department of the Bauman Maintenance and Construction Trust, where I worked at one time as a carpenter, they made the entry "Discharged on departure for Baku," and later, at the police station, it was not easy for me to prove that I had never gone to Baku.)

"Well, yes, for registration," said the building manager, beginning to get angry. "The authorization came."

The elevator to the sixth floor seemed so slow. I flew down the stairs with the passports. However, in the office I was in no hurry to give the passports to the building manager, but first asked to see the order. I turned this priceless document around in my hands for a long time and saw the entry, made on the reverse side, that my family consisted of one person.

"What do you mean, of one person?" I asked the building manager.

"What, did your wife give birth already?" he asked.

"No, she hasn't yet. But whether she gives birth or not, we're still two persons." For clarity, I showed him two fingers and winked.

"Well, you understand," said the building manager, "I'm a colonel . . . or rather, no . . . You, as head of a family—understand?—are entered on the first page. Here: Voinovich, Vladimir Nikolaevich. And here are entered the members of your family, of which you as yet have only one." And the building manager showed me one finger. "Right?"

After some hesitation, I gave him the passports and my military service card, from which the building manager learned, apparently with some disappointment, that I was just rank-and-file.

•

July 25. Everything was over. The passport registrar of the 12th precinct, breathing twice on the PERMANENTLY REGISTERED stamp, printed it on my wife's and my passports.

•

"Well," asked the elevator lady, "is he still pestering you?"

"Guess not, he apparently gave up."

"What a character, that one!" she said, almost admiringly. "He went to America, picked up those American ways. So he gave up finally. Every time I see him, he's going around so mad. Gets into the car mad, gets out of the car mad. And his wife goes around mad, doesn't talk to anybody. Oh, these Americans! Here's what I say, Vladimir Nikolaevich, it's a good thing we've got the Soviet regime. We can still get at the truth. But if it weren't for the Soviet regime, then those Americans, oi!"

The people's belief in the Soviet regime . . . But it won't alter this situation. Although a number of factors affected our victory, I would suggest the following in particular: the pregnancy of women, a unified collective, and my own stubbornness. Now that the conflict is over, I am quite content with the fact that in the future my writings won't be published; I am prepared for the Minister of Culture of the RSFSR to condemn my writings, saying that they are anti-Soviet, harmful, or simply vicious (which he did, by the way). If I were banished, though, I would invite the foreign correspondents (after all, ours wouldn't come) and turn this into an international scandal, to bring down on myself the anger of the State Security Committee. But I have brought this generally typical story to an untypically happy end. I am afraid that not everyone wanting the additional floor space would agree to subject themselves to similar risks. If the all-powerful Ivanko stood in the way of our pure-souled elevator lady (and he would not be ashamed to), I am not convinced that her faith in the beloved regime would remain steadfast.

Epilogue

Nearly two years have passed since this episode came to an end. Soon after his defeat, our respected colleague again began to appear at board meetings. He was again kind and affable, he smiled amicably at his recent enemies, he took an active part in discussions of our local problems—whether to put in new sewer pipes and whether to install trash bins on the stair landings—and, voting with everyone else for some decision or other, he modestly raised his whole hand and not just one crooked finger.

Since Turganov has ceased to be a Figure on the regional level, his stentorian voice, for some reason, has not been heard in the courtyard.

Vera Ivanovna bears herself modestly, just like her husband, the Sinologist Eidlin. I do not know if he managed to publish his Chinese novel. I think he did. Why not?

A collection of Kozlovsky's puns came out at Goslitizdat.

Crestfallen, Colonel Emyshev stole two hundred rubles of state funds, but, caught red-handed, he was forced to return them and leave work in order to avoid more serious consequences. Despite the losses he had borne since '32.

Boris Gribanov, as indicated earlier, was overseas for a time, where he publicized our literature. I don't know how successfully.

Melentiev became Minister of Culture of the RSFSR.

Nor did our respected colleague stay too long in his previous office. Transferring to a job in the Ministry of Foreign Affairs, he went to the United States for another six-year stint. Before leaving, they say he called our new chairman, said goodbye, he regretted what had happened, Turganov had pulled him into the affair and discredited him before the collective. (You see, Turganov was to blame for everything. It was he who jerked our respected colleague's strings and said in his voice: They'll dance to my tune yet.) Now our respected colleague represents our great country at the United Nations. I don't know how he does it exactly. Does he hold up to ridicule Israeli militarism, speak in defense of Greek prisoners, disclose the aggressive purposes of the NATO bloc? I believe, however, that he still has a bit of time and money left to prowl around the Manhattan shops for new equipment for his little nest. After all, we live in a rapidly changing world, and it is certainly possible that the previous equipment has already become obsolete. Perhaps in Manhattan they're selling toilets of the latest design. What kind? My fancy is insufficient to imagine what they can think up over in the West. Perhaps some sort of stereophonic toilet, or one that turns the raw materials it devours into pure gold. What won't they come up with in the West for the sake of profit!

We are completing our portrait. Its artistic originality lies in the fact that the hero appears simultaneously in a natural naked state and in a hat with a straight brim, in his own political machine and in his personal car, in the circle of his protectors, the circle of his minions, the circle of his family, and the circle of his belongings. He is one character in many. He simultaneously speaks at a high rostrum and sits at a session of the Executive Committee, passes sentence on someone in court and writes a satirical article in the newspaper concerning the periodic intensification of the class struggle.

But, strangely enough, he fights against precisely what he himself strives for in all his designs. Parasite of parasites, in a loud voice that drowns out the others, he sings, "Parasites, never!" He fights against manifestations of Philistine psychology, but who is more Philistine than he? He criticizes the bourgeois way of life, doing everything he can to live precisely in a bourgeois manner. He exposes toadyism toward the West, but grabs at anything that bears a foreign label. They say ideology prevents him from changing. If only it were so! Is he one to check his every step with Marx? Wouldn't the portrait come out too rose-colored? No, perhaps to us the image of our hero seems completely different. He put Marx out of his head when he passed the last test in Marxism, and that was a long time ago. He needs Marxism as a screen he can hide behind. Give him a different screen and he'll use that.

The only ideology he worships is the maximum satisfaction of his personal needs; and his needs are infinite and in conflict with his resources, which, no matter how great, are always limited. His practical activity is directed at constant expansion of these resources. And in this he is no dogmatist, no orthodox man. He's in step with the times, he mimics and adapts himself to new conditions.

What's more, he creates these conditions himself. And of course he doesn't need a free press and all those bourgeois freedoms, as he calls them. With a free press, could he possibly have even thought of undertaking such an affair? With freedom of artistic expression, could he possibly be called any sort of writer? And what would he do on his committee with these same freedoms? Would he publish Turganov? Or Kozlovsky? Why, his whole committee would go broke. Perhaps he needs free exchange of people? Why? After all, right now he offers only himself in the capacity of exchangeable human resources. And with a free exchange, someone else might go. And free exchange of ideas? He has a whole string of ideas about where he can grab what, but they, it seems, are not suitable for exchange.

No, of course, there is something else. Dogmatic Marxism, ideological arguments with China, economic problems, etc.

When you examine the principal factors of our story and attempt to find and explain the reasons for great social changes—such things as collectivization, industrialization, and cultural revolution, or the struggle against political deviation, religious prejudices, Trotskyism, Cubism, cosmopolitanism, Weismannism, Morganism, modernism, and contemporary revisionism—do not overlook the humble drudge with the simple, unmemorable, greedy face. Gentle, smiling, obliging, efficient, ready to do you a good turn, flatter your self-esteem, he is present in every cell of our society, breathing life into all those changes. And while you plan great reform programs, build castles in the air, search for mistakes in Hegel, create a line of poetry, or try to see an X chromosome through a microscope, our humble drudge, with his sharp little eyes, watches carefully to see if, under the guise of struggling against alien ideology, he can get something from you: an apartment, a wife, a cow, an invention, a position, an academic title. Gradually, in leisurely fashion, he heats up the atmosphere, and then you notice, on his humble face, not a smile but a wolfish grin.

Before leaving the Soviet Union, the novelist Viktor Nekrasov wrote a letter about the condition of our culture, about the fact that many honest and talented people are subjected to senseless badgering and are forced to leave the country where they were born and grew up, which they served, and without which life is inconceivable.

"Who needs this system?" Nekrasov asked.

Well, just take our hero for example, Sergei Sergeevich Ivanko.

He needs it!

1973–5

APPENDIX

Before turning this book over to be published, I circulated it from hand to hand to increase our community's awareness of the problems discussed. Soon after, I received the first letter from one of my readers. Although apparently it is not the custom to print letters from readers of a work side by side with the work itself, I decided to include this letter in my book, for, in my opinion, it distinctly adds to the portrait of our hero.

My very dear Vladimir Nikolaevich!
I read your *Ivankiad* and felt like writing you. I also read *Chonkin* just a while ago. Your choice of hero—first Ivan Chonkin, then Ivanko—reflects your closeness to folk sources and your ability to get to the root of the matter. Many problems touched upon in these two books disturb me; for example, why did work create man from apes and not from horses? Or your question: Can a saucepan be considered a member of the Writers' Union? And you answer, very resourcefully in my opinion, that it is impossible for a saucepan to be considered a writer, though it may of course be a member of the Writers' Union.

But today I took up the pen not only as a grateful reader of your cheerful and witty books; I write you because I was fortunate enough to become entangled with the characters of *The Ivankiad*. You related how Chukovsky's granddaughter came to Ivanko to plead for the publication of *Chukokkala*. Well, I am she herself, and I was just itching to add a few more strokes to the monumental portrait of your hero. But, more importantly, it is about *Chukokkala* that I have something to add.

The thing is that your respected colleague Sergei

Sergeevich Ivanko played a very appreciable—I would even venture to say, decisive—role in the history of *Chukokkala*. But before turning our floodlight on him, I must digress and explain first what *Chukokkala* is.

Chukokkala, Kornei Chukovsky's miscellanea, was begun in 1914 and existed for more than half a century. The following poets contributed to the miscellanea: Anna Akhmatova, Alexander Blok, Ivan Bunin, Nikolai Gumilev, Osip Mandelstam, Vladimir Mayakovsky, Nikolai Oleinikov, Boris Pasternak, Vladislav Khodasevich, Velimir Khlebnikov; the prosaists: Leonid Andreev, Arkady Averchenko, Isaac Babel, Maxim Gorky, Evgeny Zamyatin, Mikhail Zoshchenko, Yuri Olesha, Boris Pilnyak, Mikhail Prishvin, Alexei Remizov, Alexei Tolstoy, Yuri Tynyanov, Evgeny Shvarts, Vyacheslav Shishkov. These artists did drawings: Yuri Annenkov, Mstislav Dobuzhinsky, Boris Grigoriev, Ilya Repin, and Sergei Chekhonin. Singers and actors also contributed to the miscellanea: Sobinov and Chaliapin, Meyerhold, Evreinov, and Kachalov. There are even a few famous Englishmen represented in *Chukokkala:* there is an inscription by Oscar Wilde, a gift from Ronald Ross (an unpublished variant of four lines from *The Ballad of Reading Gaol*), and inscriptions by H. G. Wells and Arthur Conan Doyle. Of course, I have not listed all of *Chukokkala*'s contributors; for example, I deliberately omitted the names of those who are still alive and, so to speak, able to stand up for themselves.

It is very difficult to describe the contents of the miscellanea in a few words. There are poems, prose writings, caricatures, documents (newspaper clippings, advertisements), parodies of the minutes of meetings in publishing houses, of official anniversaries and writers' conferences. "The chief characteristic of *Chukokkala* is humor," wrote Kornei Chukovsky in his foreword to the proposed edition of the book. However, one could name yet another characteristic—*Chukokkala* contains the essence of the atmosphere of that period which chaotically and fortuitously filled its pages. This is precisely what Yuri Olesha had in mind when he wrote in *Chukokkala* on February 9, 1930: "We must write confessions and not novels. More important than any novel—the most important work of the thirties will be *Chukokkala*."

At first, the publication of *Chukokkala* went well. Sevastianov, then director of Iskusstvo Publishers, came to visit Kornei Chukovsky at Peredelkino and asked him to grant his firm the right to publish this unique miscellanea. The best workers were recruited to prepare *Chukokkala* for publication. I will omit the name here, but believe me, the most qualified photographer in the world made the negatives (it was to be a facsimile edition). Blok's handwriting and Chekhonin's caricatures, all of this was supposed to be reproduced in print from offset negatives, over which (after long months of photographing the miscellanea) marvelous engravers and retouchers labored for more than a year. The work was time-consuming; over six hundred reproductions from the miscellanea were included in the book. Kornei Chukovsky worked on the commentary to the writings and drawings; ahead there was still the very complicated design and layout of the book, and then the setting in three type sizes (one for the inscriptions, another for Chukovsky's commentary, a third for the footnotes). I cannot even list all the problems we managed to overcome successfully in preparing the miscellanea for print.

I must confess that all this work cost not only time and effort but piles of money. According to figures from authoritative sources, about seventeen thousand rubles were invested in the publication.

But then, finally, everything was ready, the text of the commentary was set, proofs of the six hundred reproductions were returned to the printer, the layout of the book was put together, and there remained only to print the copies—the book was just about to come out. *Literaturnaya Gazeta* announced this happy news (March 29, 1972), and the commercial for *Chukokkala* flashed rather frequently on movie and television screens.

But suddenly, across the miscellanea's smooth path arose your respected colleague Sergei Sergeevich Ivanko, chief editor of the literary editorial board of the State Committee on Publishing, in charge of all belles lettres in all the publishing houses of the Soviet Union.

This great literary connoisseur ordered *Chukokkala* brought to him for review.

The scene you described in *The Ivankiad* of my visit to Ivanko is accurate; however, you idealize the actual situation somewhat. Alas, alas, I was unable to overcome the vigilance of the secretaries of the State Committee or Sergei Sergeevich's occupation with very important matters of state. Only in dreams can meetings with such high-placed personages as Ivanko actually occur. In reality, Sergei Sergeevich would only occasionally answer the phone and inform me: Yes, I have *Chukokkala*, but I have absolutely no time to read it and [I add this myself, as I sensed from his tone] no desire, it's not worth the trouble. Thus, my ingratiating calls and Ivanko's idle excuses dragged on from month to month. There was a new director at Iskusstvo Publishers, K. Dolgov, and at the printer's it was necessary to take apart the type for the already composed commentary and the text of the inscriptions—the storage deadline had passed. But still Ivanko dragged his feet, didn't read it, went away, came back, went to meetings, and then one day . . .

I think it was on April 25, 1973. The next time I called him, I heard something new: "We can't publish *Chukokkala* because the ceiling fell in at the printer's and the plates are broken. I promised to look at the book, but now I can't."

The news about the ceiling crushed me—just think, the marvelous contributors to the miscellanea, the editors, photographers, designers, engravers, retouchers, the offset negatives, years of work, seventeen thousand rubles, all buried in plaster. I lost my head and almost cried over the phone. I begged Ivanko to inform me exactly what was ruined and what remained intact. It seemed to me that Sergei Sergeevich was touched by my despair. In any case, he promised to request a list of the losses and to inform me of them if I would call him in two weeks. However, in two weeks, the list had not yet been supplied to him, but he again said that there had been an accident at the printer's, some chemicals had been spilled, and for that reason it was impossible to publish *Chukokkala*.

After I hung up the phone, I got to thinking. What a strange printing office, I thought. It is probably in some sort of wretched basement where half-rotten beams support cracked ceilings and all kinds of chemicals can drip through. How horrible that *Chukokkala* landed in a place like that. But how did Iskusstvo Publishers ever manage to protect the rest of its books from these natural calamities? Inquisitiveness led me further and further and, one fine day, led me to the gates of the Red Proletariat Press, where, I had finally learned, *Chukokkala* was being printed.

Those who have ever stepped through its gates will remember the steel-reinforced floors, the enclosed stairwells, the expanse of the huge workshops. And those who have not will have to take my word, because it's not so easy to pass through those gates. I managed it with some cunning. Like a wolf in sheep's clothing, I slipped into the printing office and explained my unexpected visit thus: Well, you've had an accident here and I've come to help you, save you some time; I'll quickly sort out what exactly is intact, I have been familiar with all of it since I was a child. I expected them to respond—yes, *Chukokkala*, plaster, chemicals. However, they looked at me benevolently, but with complete serenity and some amazement. I was still prattling that I wanted to help sort it out, that I wasn't afraid of work, and that I would sit over it day and night if only the business would move faster. The typesetters looked more and more suspicious, and finally one of them asked what exactly the matter was, what accident, why anyone should have to sit up day and night, and why I had come at all and taken them away from their work. And then I made a false move.

"I was told that your ceiling had collapsed and several of the *Chukokkala* negatives were damaged."

"Who told you?"

"The State Committee on Publishing."

They instantly lost interest in the subject, and everything became clear to me. I left the printing office determined never again to turn to your hero—Sergei Sergeevich Ivanko.

It's annoying, of course, that I wasted so much time on telephone calls to him. The elevator lady in your building understood what sort of character he was much faster than I. She noticed that he even brought a sled from America. And we've known for a long time what you can expect from a man who will sit in someone else's sled.*

* The Russian expression "*sadit'sya ne v svoi sani*" ("to sit in someone else's sled") means "to be out of one's depth."

Here I would have had to put an end to the whole history of *Chukokkala*, but *The Ivankiad* showed me that there was one appeal I had overlooked in my efforts on the miscellanea's behalf. And it is the only appeal that managed to gain a victory over Sergei Sergeevich Ivanko and his high-placed patrons. I have in mind the General Assembly of the Shareholders of the Moscow Writers' Cooperative.

I had rushed around everywhere, I had fussed and fussed about *Chukokkala*. It's a long list: I wrote letters to V. M. Ozerov, Secretary of the Writers' Union and member of the Commission on Kornei Chukovsky's Literary Heritage, to P. N. Demichev, Secretary of the Central Committee of the CPSU, and to B. Stukalin, President of the State Committee on Publishing; I called B. Turkin, now in Ivanko's place on the same committee; I went to Iskusstvo Publishers. Somehow, nothing happened. Of course, the persons and institutions listed were in favor of publishing the book. But still, understand me—in a few months, on March 11, 1976, it will be *ten years* since the agreement with the publishing house was first signed and the book submitted to the editors. That's no joke—ten years of intense work, struggle, and daring. The years pass, my powers weaken, and the project still lacks something—not the composition exactly, nor the binding, nor the dust jacket; in short, I don't really know what.

Then, not long ago, this summer, a new director (the third) arrived at Iskusstvo Publishers (I forgot to tell you that Sevastianov and Dolgov stepped up to higher rungs on the official ladder). So the new director arrived: Vishnyakov. About two weeks after he began work, I went to a reception at his home. Naturally, he is in favor of publishing *Chukokkala*, too. But until now, unfortunately, he hasn't had time to read it. And later he told me, for some reason lowering his voice just slightly, that next year they expect problems with paper. There will be a paper shortage. And now the printing office is demanding a fine from Iskusstvo because of the delays on *Chukokkala.* But he'll try to settle everything and call me in two weeks. He even took down my phone number.

More than two months have passed since that conversation and he still hasn't called. Things are probably very bad with the paper shortage.

When my grandfather, Kornei Chukovsky, gave me his miscellanea *Chukokkala* in 1965, he wrote an inscription on the flyleaf which ends with the words, ". . . she [that is I] may do with it, the miscellanea, whatever she thinks best."

And I had thought best, I had this ridiculous idea stuck in my head—to publish this book in the homeland of its marvelous contributors and its compiler and creator. No matter what.

I read your *Ivankiad*, Vladimir Nikolaevich, and I came up with a new plan. What if I, in the name of several contributors to the miscellanea—let's say, Mayakovsky, Repin, Chaliapin, Alexei Tolstoy, Gorky (I'll choose those who will be the most impressive to the authorities)—what if I, in their name, were to appeal to the shareholders of the Moscow Writers' Housing Cooperative? In these years I've come to the conclusion that residential cooperatives and house managers are capable of directing the publication of books just as well as the Committee on Publishing. I shall draft a statement like the following to your residential cooperative:

> In the name of the numerous contributors to the miscellanea *Chukokkala* [the list of contributors at the

beginning of my letter] I ask that you recover from Sergei Sergeevich Ivanko, member of your cooperative, the sum of seventeen thousand rubles, wasted because of his delay in approving *Chukokkala* for publication. The sum indicated is required for payment of a fine imposed by the printing office in connection with the long storage of the negatives and also for compensation for expenditures on the discarded matter from the text of the book.

Bearing in mind the services of the miscellanea's contributors to Russian culture, and also considering the official awards to the miscellanea's compiler—the much-decorated Kornei Chukovsky, Lenin Prize Laureate, Doctor of Literature Emeritus of Oxford University *honoris causa*—I request that the General Assembly of the Shareholders of the Moscow Writers' Housing Cooperative announce a paper drive among the tenants to provide pulp for the future publication of *Chukokkala*.

What do you think, Vladimir Nikolaevich, would it be worthwhile to submit such a statement? It seems to me that if the housing cooperative approached the proposal I have put forward constructively, it would be possible to overcome the obstacle that is sitting in the way of publication.

Ivanko probably won't bother about the money, anyway. After all, he's saved a lot since he didn't have to break through a main wall, buy Bazhova a one-room apartment, equip yet another room, etc. And I don't think pulp will be a problem either these days.

Dear Vladimir Nikolaevich! Forgive me for asking you to shoulder this new worry—fussing about *Chukokkala* at the housing cooperative board. But then, as you know, new victories are expected of those who have already won. And perhaps, thanks to your *Ivankiad,* the long-suffering and patient reader will at last, one fine day, open *Chukokkala* and read on its pages verse and prose, as yet unknown to him, by the illustrious champions of our immortal and fragile, eternal and transient Russian culture.

Regards,
Elena Chukovskaya